THUGLIT

Issue Eighteen

Edited by Todd Robinson

These are works of fiction. Names, characters, corporations, institutions, organizations, events, or locales in the works are either the product of the author's imagination or, if real, used fictitiously. The resemblance of any character to actual persons (living or dead) is entirely coincidental.

THUGLIT: Issue Eighteen
ISBN-13:978-1514743393
ISBN-10:1514743396

Published by THUGLIT Publishing.

Table of Contents

A Message from Big Daddy Thug

Ahoy-hoy, Thugleteers!

I learned this past week the darkest pits of mankind's suffering.

The depth of pain that humanity can sink into, curled up into a ball like a mewling kitten that has been impaled on a shish kabob skewer…

What is this, you ask? What with the stories you publish, many of them featuring characters and acts that would make the Marquis de Sade defile his pantaloons and run screaming like a terrified Daffy Duck—what could possibly make Big Daddy Thug gnash his teeth and pray for a quick death?

Kidney stones, my brothers and sisters.

Holy Hell… Those little crystalline bastards are noir as fuck. At various times in my pain-filled existence, I've been maced, whacked in the noggin with a blackjack, stabbed with a broken beer bottle, and t-boned by a Cadillac right on the driver's side door. And lemme tell you…kidney stones win. Like I said—noir as fuck.

So, extra thanks go out to Lady Detroit for her editing acumen, taking the reins at the end from my trembling mitts, and riding this bitch of a magazine through the finish line—all the while restraining herself from smothering my groans of pain with a pillow over the face.

She's a hell of a lady.

And at almost the ten-year mark, Thuglit has still never, EVER missed a deadline…although we sure as fuck came close here. I just kept repeating our deadline motto:

Neither snow nor rain nor heat nor rocks coming out of our pee-pees will stay these editors from the swift completion of their beloved THUGLIT.

Hope you dig the ish for it's on-timedness as much as for the content within. Maybe more, this time out.

Meanwhile, I'll just be over here on the floor in a fetal position while Lady Detroit eyeballs those pillows…

IN THIS ISSUE OF THUGLIT:

- Finders keepers.
- Hot for teacher.
- Some people deserve a good robbin'
- Sometimes, dead is betta! (My apologies to Stephen King…and everyone from Maine.)
- Good help is hard to find.
- Fair is foul and foul is fair.
- Wrestling is fake, until it isn't…
- M-I-C! K-E-Y! Please don't suuu-uuuue meeeee!

SEE YOU IN 60, FUCKOS!!! (maybe)
Todd Robinson (Big Daddy Thug) 6/30/2015

Waylon, On Rerun

by Michael Pool

Waylon had already loaded up the microwave, the DVD player, a desktop computer and half the food in the fridge when the aging, mentally challenged man showed up at the chain-link fence that lined the back alley behind the house.

"Hi," the man said, squinting against the sun as Waylon moved past him to the back of his pumpkin-colored van. "This is Mr. Collins' house?"

Waylon nodded, even though he had no idea whose house it was. He tried to figure in his head whether or not the retarded grey-haired man he recognized from the thrift store a few blocks over would be able to identify him later. Maybe. But the goddamn television was heavy, and he couldn't move it by himself. The pock-skinned man stared off down the alley like a child might.

"What's your name there, partner?" Waylon asked.

The man did an about-face like Waylon had learned in ROTC back in high school, before he discovered heroin out on the rodeo circuit.

"Oh. I'm Bernie. Are you here helping Mr. Collins too?"

"You bet."

"Wanna know what?"

"What's that, bub?"

"You should get a mohawk, shawty." Bernie pointed at Waylon's shaggy hair.

Waylon sighed. Bernie had said the same thing when Waylon came through his line at the thrift store with some second-hand clothes a few weeks back, the day after he got out of the klink this last time. It had taken at least ten minutes for Bernie to ring him up. Enough time to tell the same two jokes four times each. Someone who volunteered there must have taught Bernie to use the term "shawty," without telling him what it meant.

"You think so?" Waylon said, keeping his voice friendly.

"Aww, I'm just jokin'," Bernie hollered, then grinned to reveal a mouth with half the teeth missing.

"What can I say, Bernie? You got me. Anyway, my name's Charlie Daniels, and Mr. Collins told me to ask for your help."

"Mr. Collins says I'm a good helper."

"Well it's my lucky day then, Bernie, because I could use a strong fella like you to help move his television set into the van here."

"Because Mr. Collins don't want to watch no more?" Bernie asked.

"Well—ah—not exactly. I wanna borrow it from him, but I can't carry it by myself."

"But how will he watch shows? I watch lots of shows."

Waylon forced a smile. "I guess he'll have to manage. Anyhow, could you come inside and give me a hand?"

"Sure thing, shawty."

"You are a good helper, Bernie."

"Missus Collins says God made me to be a helper."

"Well, she must be real proud of you then. Follow me, bubba." Waylon walked through the garage into the kitchen, which he'd torn apart looking for stashed money, then into the living room. Bernie stayed just behind him on his heels.

"The television is right over—"

"Ding-dong the witch is dead! Ding-dong the witch is dead! Ding-dong!" Bernie screamed, jumping up and down and

pointing at something over Waylon's left shoulder. Waylon followed Bernie's eyes to a set of commemorative plates for *The Wizard of Oz* arranged on a built-in bookshelf. One of them had the Wicked Witch of the West's green face painted on it. Bernie's eyes swelled to the size of jawbreakers. Bernie pointed at the plate and shuffled his hips like he needed to pee.

"It's just a plate, Bernie, calm down," Waylon said.

Bernie's face turned bright red. *"Ding-dong,"* he sang again. "I don't like the witch. She sets the Scarecrow on fire. Then shawty comes and throws the bucket of water all over The Witch, and she melts like ice cream. I'm glad she melted."

"Well I'm glad too, Bernie." Waylon walked over to the plate and set it flat, so that the face was no longer visible. "I'll tell you what. You like the Scarecrow?"

"Yeah. I like for him to dance."

"Well look at this." Waylon reached up to the top shelf, took a plate down with the Scarecrow painted on the center of it, caught mid-way through some sort of jig. "Mr. Collins has got a plate with the Scarecrow on it too. He said if you help me move the television out, it's yours."

"Really?" Bernie asked, the Wicked Witch gone from his mind now. "I can take it home?"

"You can take it home, eat dinner off of it, whatever you want."

"I can't use that for eating, but I could just look at it I guess."

"Hell Bernie, you can give it a mohawk if that's what you want. But for now, let's just get the television moved. I'm running a little late."

"But don't forget to let me have the plate after."

"I won't forget. Deal? Now if you'll just get the other side of this television…there you go, and now on a count of three we can lift it together and carry it out. Ready? One—two—three."

They lifted the television together. Waylon swung around so that he would be the one moving backwards as they took the television up the two steps into the kitchen toward the back door.

They made it up the steps and were halfway to the back door when Bernie dropped his end without warning, brought his wrists up to his armpits like wings and yelled *"Cockadoodledoo!"* He flapped his bent elbows up and down like a rooster. Waylon yelped and dropped his end too. The set landed right on Waylon's foot, and he knew without looking that both were probably broken. He gasped as a throbbing pain shot up his leg to his spine.

"Goddammit Bernie," Waylon yelled, hopping on his good foot now. "Goddammit goddammit. You stupid son-of-a-bitch. I think you broke my fucking foot. You definitely broke the TV."

Bernie looked horrified, but kept glancing beyond Waylon at the ceramic rooster on top of the fridge, almost reaching up as if to flap his wings more, then stopping and sinking back into the horrified look again. His lip quivered and his eyes welled up. Waylon wished right away he'd not let his temper go like that.

"I'm…I'm sorry," Bernie mumbled, "I didn't mean to drop the television. I'm so stupid." He repeated the last part again and then slapped himself across the face, hard. Then again. He threw himself to the ground next to the cratered television set and started banging his head against the linoleum floor. He'd already managed to leave a series of welts and splits in his forehead, as well as deep hand marks on his cheeks, before Waylon could shimmy over to try and make him stop,.

"*Stupid, Stupid, Stupid,*" Bernie said. "I don't know why I'm so stupid."

"Hey, just take it easy," Waylon said, trying to sound authoritative. He tried to restrain Bernie's hands, but Bernie was much stronger than he looked. Bernie ripped his hands away and continued to go to town on himself, until finally Waylon said fuck it and bowled him over flat on his back. He sat on Bernie's chest like a horse. "Relax Bernie. RELAX," he said, pinning Bernie's arms to the floor.

Bernie squirmed and struggled. He didn't seem to want or be able to calm down. Waylon didn't want to hit him, but he couldn't afford to waste much more time. He needed to get Bernie under control, collect anything of remaining value, and get out. Bernie was slobbering and moaning, yanking at his arms more like he wanted to hit himself again than get free. Waylon held him down as best he could, not sure what else to do.

"What in God's name are you two doing in my house?" a gruff voice said behind Waylon. "My God. Bernie, is that you?"

"Hello Mr. Collins," Bernie replied, shifting gears in an instant, no longer struggling under Waylon's grip now. "I came to help after church, like you said. I could give you a mohawk now if you want? Just jokin'!"

"So you are, and so I see," the old man said, his voice barely able to hide the rage on his face, but maybe attempting to do so for Bernie's sake. "Mister," he added, "I don't know who you are or why you're in my house, but you'd best get off Bernie there before Mora comes in and—"

"Before I come in and what?" A woman's head with a daisy-topped straw hat appeared just over the old man's shoulder. She shrieked when she noticed Waylon sitting on Bernie. "Bernie," she said, her startled eyes taking in the scene, the busted television, emptied cabinets, everything really. "What are you doing to my sweet, sweet Bernie?"

Waylon had never felt so low. He released Bernie's arms and started to stand up. Though her husband seemed to be in shock, Mora didn't have the same problem.

"You were abusing Bernie," she screamed. "How could you? He's—special. You're a monster."

"Now just hold up, ma'am," Waylon tried to explain as he moved to stand up. "He was hitting hisself and—" Before Waylon could finish, the woman snatched the ceramic rooster from top of the fridge and swung it with both hands like a sledgehammer. The rooster shattered against the side of Waylon's face and he crumbled to the ground, unconscious.

Waylon came to with a splitting headache and blood running down his face. He tried to reach up and massage his temples, but discovered his hands were bound behind his back instead. He remembered where he was then. His eyes wouldn't focus for a moment. When they finally did focus, he was staring straight into the long chrome barrel of a .357 pistol.

"You just stay still and take it easy there mister," said Mr. Collins, who Waylon recognized now as the manager of the thrift store where he'd first seen Bernie.

"I don't think I could move if I tried," Waylon replied.

"That's good. You probably wouldn't live long enough to try anything else if you did. Police are on their way. In the meantime, maybe you'd like to explain how you came to find yourself abusing a poor, mentally-handicapped man like Bernie in my house?"

"I don't guess I've got much to say," Waylon replied.

Collins cocked the hammer on the pistol and poked Waylon in the forehead with the barrel's tip. "Still got nothing to say?"

Waylon sighed and let his shoulders slump. "Okay, I get your drift. What can I say? I was robbing the place when Bernie showed up at the back fence. I knew it was stupid when I done it, but I couldn't carry the television by myself. Goddamn thing's so old I probably couldn't have gotten twenty bucks for it anyway, with all these flat-screens around these days. Fact remains, I needed that twenty. So I got Bernie to help me carry the television out. Except he dropped it. Apparently he's got a thing for roosters."

Collins released the hammer and let the gun's barrel pan down to the floor. Waylon took a deep breath.

"You some kind of addict, or just an idiot?" Collins asked. "Because those are the only two reasons why I can imagine a man robbing a house in broad daylight. Given that you got Bernie involved, I'm assuming it's probably a combination of the two."

"When you're right, you're right, I reckon," Waylon said, measuring his words. "But I want ya'll to know something. I wasn't hurting Bernie. I might be a thief, but I ain't no bully. My daddy bout whipped me to death way back when, and I'd never lay my hands on someone like that. After Bernie dropped your television, he got all worked up and started whipping on hisself. I was trying to stop him when ya'll come in and jacked me up with the rooster." Waylon wanted to rub his head where the rooster had connected.

"I see. Well, he's been known to do that, unfortunate though it is. I think it's probably pretty frustrating being Bernie, wouldn't you say? I hope you're happy, though. This whole thing's scared the daylights out of him. Mora's back there trying to calm him down now. Not to mention you've destroyed our home."

"I get it, I do. I'm actually surprised you didn't shoot my dumb ass, though I'm thankful. I'm sorry for all this, really I am. Truth is, I'm a junkie. It's a hell of a thing. I just can't keep my country ass off the dope. Even sitting here right now, feeling like the low-down piece of shit that I am, part of me's thinking whether or not I'll be able to score a hit in county lockup. The answer is maybe. I know you probably don't want to hear that, but it's the truth."

"There's a certain irony to it, Mr...I didn't catch your name?"

"Name's Waylon Tompkins. I'd say pleased to meet you, but I don't want to feed ya'll any more bullshit today."

"Mr. Tompkins," Collins said, as if trying out his name. "Waylon. I understand you more than you think, Waylon Tompkins. As it happens, my son Jacob died from a heroin overdose. Only way Mora and I managed to survive it was to make our mission in life to help addicts. Addicts, and also some of the mentally handicapped, though someone watching us here right now might say there's not much difference in the two when it comes to decision making."

"Yeah, they might say that, I guess," Waylon said.

"Now let me give you some truth. I'd like to help you too, Waylon." Collins using his first name now, getting comfortable with him. "From where I'm standing, a person has to be out of their mind with sickness to trick a mentally disabled man into helping him rob the home of people who would give him the shirts off their backs anyway. The only people around town who provide work, shelter and stability for a man like Bernie. And also for a man like yourself."

Waylon frowned, still wanting to rub his swollen head. "Had I known it, I would've picked someplace else."

"You see, that's just it, Waylon. There is no place else. It's all one place. That you would victimize anyone is a sign of a deep upheaval within yourself. I'd like to help you rectify that, if you decide you want to try."

"So you're not gonna press charges, then?" Waylon asked, hopeful.

"I didn't say that, Waylon. Accountability is the currency of civilization. You've accrued a debt, now you'll have make things whole again. But once you get free from that, if you want to, you could come work at the shop and stay at our shelter. So long as you stay clean and work our program."

Waylon started to reply, but someone pounded on the front door and they both looked up instead.

"Looks like your ride's here. Let's get you up and at em." Collins kept the gun in his right hand and grasped Waylon's inner bicep with the left. He helped Waylon to his feet. "You just remember what I said, Waylon Tompkins. We run The Lord's Salvation Thrift Store here in town. You pay your debt and want to stay clean, then you come see us."

"I might just do that," Waylon said, knowing it was another lie even as he said it.

Collins led him by the arm into the living room just as his wife Mora opened the door to reveal two police officers, each with a hand on his pistol. Both cops glared at Waylon before the bigger one, who had a thick moustache, spoke.

"Get facedown on the ground," he said. "Now."

Waylon complied as best he could with his hands bound, dropped to his knees and then lay facedown like the man instructed. Collins guided him by the arm all the way to the ground, then let go and stepped back.

"We found him in the kitchen," Collins said. "He's got a van back in the alley with some of our stuff in it, too."

The cops stepped up and flanked Waylon on either side. Waylon winced when they each drove a knee into his kidneys. They replaced whatever had been used to bind his hands with a set of handcuffs instead, then yanked him to his feet by the cuffs.

"Shit, man, ouch," Waylon said. "I'm compliant. Ya'll don't have to be so rough about it."

The mustached cop slapped him upside the head. "Stop resisting," he said.

"Easy there, gentlemen," Collins said. "No need for that. I think he's had enough for today."

Neither of the cops replied, but they didn't hit Waylon again, either. Instead they led him toward the front door.

"Does this mean I don't get the Scarecrow?" Bernie said from behind him. Waylon craned his neck around so that he could just see the edge of Bernie's tear-streaked face poking out the bathroom door.

"That ain't up to me now, bub," Waylon said. "I'm sorry I got you into this mess, though. I get out, I'll bring you a Scarecrow plate, up at your work. Sound okay?" Another lie.

Bernie seemed to be waiting for permission from Collins to speak. The old man nodded his head.

"Okay, shawty. Sorry about the television. I guess you won't get to watch your shows now either."

Waylon knew they had cable in county lockup, but figured this wasn't the time to bring it up. "I guess not," he said instead.

"You come see us when you get out," Collins said. Waylon nodded as the cops moved him out the front door again.

"When you bring the plate I could give you a mohawk," Bernie said.

"I suppose you could, Bernie," Waylon called over his shoulder, thinking how the old woman had already pretty damn much given him one.

"I'm just jokin'!" Bernie said.

As the officers led Waylon out to the backseat of a cruiser parked at the curb, he couldn't help wondering if it was the truth.

Proof of Death

by Mike Madden

I take a deep drag, unleash a billowing cloud and kick my feet up on the credenza. The client lifts the nameplate off my desk. That plate is an antique, a family heirloom, a fifty-year-old brass block inscribed *Law Office of Joseph Skelter*. And it's mine. I launch another cloud across the desk and he sets it down, his face registering mild annoyance at the vapor.

Dad fired up a filterless Camel whenever he wanted to unnerve a client. In Grandpa's day it was stogies, cheap South American coronas that gave tear gas a run for the money. These days it's e-cigs.

World's gone to hell.

The client is a twinkie of a man, barely five feet tall with pasty skin and a bad case of the dweebs. My first impression? In his forty-some odd years on this planet, this yahoo never committed anything worse than speeding. So why all of a sudden is he desperate to hire a criminal defense attorney? He called this morning, practically cried when my assistant told him we didn't take appointments on Saturdays.

Trixie's got a soft spot for dweebs.

"Arthur Brennan," the dweeb announces, taking a seat without offering his hand.

I stare him down.

"Ummm….my name is—"

"Whadaya want, Artie? Why are you here?"

"Well, quite frankly, I'm in need of an experienced attorney and," he adds this last part with gusto, "I don't care what it costs."

Heard that line a hundred times. And what I've learned the hard way is, when a client says they don't care what it costs, it usually means they have no intention of paying.

"How about this," I tell him. "We skip the part where I rape you with fees and get right to the part where you tell me what the hell is going on."

Brennan flashes angry, then slides back into his humble demeanor. "I hardly know where to begin. There was just so much…blood."

It's a scientific fact. Certain phrases in the English language have the capacity to drop the temperature in a room five degrees. "My husband is pulling into the driveway," for example. "There was just so much blood," is good for ten. Heard it before, but every time it gives me a chill.

"Go on."

"Well, quite frankly, what happened was…"

"Uh huh?"

"The thing is, it all started…"

He's going to be one of those mumble-mouthed twerps that take forever to admit the deed. Lost patience for it years ago. Besides, coaxing a client to open up? Taking the time to establish rapport, slowly winning confidence while extracting the truth like a proctologist removing a delicate tumor?

Not my forte.

"What you have to understand is—"

"Trixie!" I bark into the intercom.

Brennan stiffens, as if some sadist had just yanked on the poker up his ass.

"Relax, Artie. Ms. Valero is my legal assistant and investigator. Talking to her is like talking to me. Completely confidential."

Brennan does a one-eighty when Trixie floats into the room. A short-haired brunette, she's shapely, thin, and flaunting quite the ensemble: a black skirt slit up the thigh and a tight white top under a black bolero jacket. The silk scarf I'd given her for client meetings is wrapped tightly around her neck and dangling in front like a tie.

"Ms. Valero," I say. "Mr. Brennan was just getting ready to explain his problem. Why don't you join us?"

"Certainly, Mr. Skelter. Happy to assist."

Trixie knows the routine. Gliding into the seat next to Brennan, she slips on her librarian glasses, the ones that make her look like Adrian from Rocky. Not the tight-assed frump from the pet shop either, the cute Adrian from *Rocky III*. Like most of my clients, Brennan takes an instant shine to her.

"You were saying something," I remind him. "About blood?"

"We've been having problems."

"Who's we?" asks Trixie.

"My wife and I, of course," Brennan scoffs.

Whadaya know? The dweeb draws the line at taking guff from women.

"Get it straight, little man." Trixie leans forward, working the slit in her skirt to highlight her muscle-toned thighs. "You want help? You'll answer my fuckin' questions."

Brennan looks at me aghast.

I kick back to enjoy the show.

"My wife!" he blurts, as if grabbed by the balls. "She's been working evenings, sometimes until two in the morning. I got suspicious. Who wouldn't?"

"Go on," Trixie scolds, adjusting her scarf, exposing a plunging v-neck hugging the curves of her breasts and terminating mid-cleavage.

"I lied. Told her I had a conference in Chicago. Called for car service and pretended to leave. After a few hours, I headed back. There was this beat-up clunker in my driveway. I went in the house and there they were on the couch, her and this jerk. They were…they were…"

"We get the picture." Trixie unbuttons the bolero, leaving Brennan awaiting her next move. "Keep going," she orders.

"I screamed. Cursed. Threatened the jerk! He got off the couch and came at me like he was going to—I don't know what. My wife tried to stop him. I picked up a lamp. Oh dear God! The one Mother gave us. She bought it in London when she went to visit Aunt—"

"Back to it, dammit." She tugs at the bolero, as if ready to peel it off.

"I meant to hit him. I swung and missed. Bashed her across the face. I didn't mean to do it. I just…" Brennan breaks down, sobbing like the dweeb he is.

Another proven fact. The most efficient way to extract the truth from a straight male is to have a sexy yet reserved-looking female fire questions like a drill sergeant. In my amateur opinion, it has something to do with the psychology of contrast. Sex versus reserve. Reserve verses aggression. Someone should commission a study.

"When did this happen?" Trixie demands.

"About two hours ago."

"Is she…"

"Dead?" Brennan asks, the dread in his voice unmistakable. "Well, quite frankly, I suspect she is. The jerk checked her pulse and said she was gone. I ran out of there."

Trixie eases back in her chair and gives me the nod.

"Enough," I say. "What is it, exactly, you want from us?"

"My uncle, James Delgado, told me you once helped him out one time. Said you might be able to help. Can you help me, Mr. Skelter?"

I steal a look at Trixie. James Delgado, *aka* Jimmy the Pimp, was a case we'd handled a few years back. Delgado owned a gentleman's club in Center-City Philly, a high-class strip joint that dabbled in low-class prostitution. Delgado fancied himself connected to the Mob. When they busted him, he offered to pay me by "taking care of" anyone I wanted. A few names came to mind, but I settled for cash in the end. He paid me in twenties and never brought up the subject again. Looking at Brennan, it's hard to believe he's related to a sleazeball like Delgado.

I give Trixie the signal.

"Our standard retainer agreement." Trixie spreads the papers on the desk. "Twenty-five thousand, up to and including trial. Questions?"

Brennan signs on the dotted line and writes a check without looking at the retainer. "Am I going to jail?"

"Too early to tell." I hold out my hand. "House keys."

"Why do you need—"

"We're going to swing by your place. Check out the crime scene. Don't worry, if it turns out the jerk called the cops, we'll keep rolling."

"Why wouldn't he have called the cops?"

"Might be married," Trixie explains. "Found himself in a compromising position. For all we know, he high-tailed it just like you."

"In the meantime,," I gesture for Trixie to show Brennan out, "keep a low profile. Don't go anywhere near your car. They may be looking for it. There's a coffee shop up the street. Meet you there in two hours."

Brennan follows Trixie to the door, still moping, but eyes glued to her ass the whole way.

Trixie cat-walks back into my office. She unwraps her Adam's apple scarf while doing her celebration jig. Trixie has always been a big help interviewing clients, but ever since her operation (and changing her name from Trevor Jones to Trixie Valero), she's been a real asset.

"So, Trix. Whadaya think?"

"Well, quite frankly," she leans on my desk, fanning herself with the retainer check, "he's everything a girl could want. Rich, submissive…newly single. I kinda like the little fellah."

Trixie kills me.

I figure Brennan has to be set up pretty well since he gave a Center-City address, but the place is a social climber's dream—a three-level townhouse with a circular drive in a black-tie section of Society Hill. There's no sign of police, so we let ourselves in.

The only dead body I've ever seen was at my grandfather's wake. Trixie doesn't seem fazed at all, so I do the gentlemanly thing: close my eyes and let her go first.

I brace for the shock of the scene. A dead woman on the ground. A shattered face. Bones jutting out every which—

"Joe!"

I crack my eyes. The living room rug is stained red with blood. A broken lamp on the floor. Other than that, the room is immaculate.

"Mrs. Brennan?" Trixie takes off through the living room. "Mrs. Brennan! Are you alright, dear?"

We search the house and find no sign of the wife, just cherry wood furnishings, nineteenth-century impressionist prints and a pair of padded handcuffs on the night table. The typical trappings of American well-to-do yuppiedom.

Trixie's cellphone starts singing "It's Raining Men."

Kills me.

"Trixie Valero," she answers. "What? No, Arthur. Stay off the phone. Go back to the office and wait for us there." She beeps off the cell and flashes me her you-ain't-gonna-believe-this face.

"Well?" I ask.

"Brennan got a voicemail from the Jerk."

"Get out."

"He wants Brennan to call him immediately."

"Say why?"

"Just that it would be in his...best interest."

My office is in an old Victorian on Ridge Avenue in the Roxborough section of Northwest Philly where I grew up. Far from chic, but suits me fine. Grandpa practiced law in the neighborhood for thirty years. When he died, Dad moved the practice to neighboring Manayunk to cater to the yuppies renovating the old homes along the Schuylkill River. The high rent forced him out during the real estate boom of the early 2000's and by the time I took over, we were back in the old hood. These days even Roxborough is getting uppity. Coffee houses and yoga studios are slowly replacing the corner bars and cheesesteak shops that were once the neighborhood's claim to fame.

"Scarf," I say to Trixie, as we walk up the steps to the office.

"Jeeze Louise." She tosses it around her neck. "Such a prude."

Brennan is sitting on the couch in the reception area with his face in his hands, but springs to his feet as we walk in. "Why would he call me? Did you go to the house? Were the cops there?"

"Phone." Trixie extends her palm.

Brennan slaps his cell in her hand. "Is my wife—"

"Sit." She points a finger straight down.

Brennan drops, puppy-dog style to the edge of the couch.

We head to my office. Trixie slams the door and we stand there listening to Brennan's last voicemail:

"Artie. I think you know who this is. If you want to stay out of jail, then we've got to talk. Ring me back at this number. Trust me, mate, it's in your best interest."

Trixie hits "return call" and hands me the phone.

"Ello?"

It's the same grating cockney accent as was on the voice message.

"This is Joseph Skelter," I say. "I represent Arthur Brennan. You wanted to speak with him?"

"That's right, mate."

"You can talk to me."

I let the Union Jack-off blather on for a full minute, then say, "Call you back," and hang up.

After filling Trixie in on what the Jerk said, I ask her to fetch our client.

"Good news," I tell Brennan, "is that your wife isn't home. There's a lot of blood, like you said, but no body. Which means—"

"She's not dead! Oh, thank God! Thank you, Mr. Skelter."

Trixie hangs an arm over Brennan's shoulder "Let's not start patting each other's asses just yet."

"Which means," I continue. "That the cops aren't looking for you."

"Not yet," Trixie adds.

"How do you know?"

"Because of the bad news, dear," Trixie says. "Listen."

"According to the Jerk," I tell him. "Your wife is dead and he's on his way to the Pine Barrens in South Jersey to bury the body, but hasn't called the cops and is willing to keep his mouth shut about the whole thing."

"Why would he do that?"

"For five hundred thousand. Cash."

The case is an ethical nightmare. On the one hand, I can't divulge to the cops anything Brennan told me about killing his wife. On the other hand, advising him to pay a witness to dispose of the *corpus delicti* could make me a defendant. Either way, I have to figure out what the hell is going on. I send Brennan back to the reception area to give the poor dweeb an opportunity to get a handle on his hyperventilating.

Trixie leans, arms folded, against my desk. "I don't buy it. The Jerk is engaged in a little hanky-panky with Brennan's wife."

"Check."

"Next thing he knows, he's witnessing a murder."

"Check."

"But he has the presence of mind, in the middle of all that, to concoct this body-snatch, extortion scheme?"

"Hmmm."

"This ain't got the right scent, Joe."

"Sure it does. What happened is—"

"Obvious." Trixie goes into figure-it-out mode, pacing back and forth behind the desk. "Brennan catches his wife and the Jerk doing the hunka-chunka on the couch, then he whacks her with the lamp, *bam!*"

"Hunka-chunka?"

"He starts to make the 911 call, but before he gets through, Mrs. Brennan wakes up. Turns out she wasn't dead, merely knocked out. The Jerk drops the phone and gets this five-hundred-thousand-dollar grin as it occurs to him they can blackmail Brennan."

"Ridiculous," I say. "The wife would never go for it. Brennan is worth at least twice that much. Why not just divorce the twerp, take half and avoid the felony extortion charges?"

"Because…" Trixie holds up a finger, then plops in my chair. "…I dunno, but I still think we need proof of death," she says. "We demand to see the body."

"No way."

"Why not?"

"The Jerk thinks he stands to gain half a million if Brennan believes she's dead. Whadaya think he's gonna do if she's alive and we demand proof of death? It's like asking him to whack her."

"Fine. A picture, then."

"Come on. You don't think he can stage a pic?"

"Let him." She kicks her pumps up on the desk, throws her hands behind her head and flashes me a grin. "Be surprised what you can learn from a pic."

At this point, I figure it can't hurt. I hit the Jerk's number and put it on speaker.

"Ello?"

"Look here, Ringo. We may be able to work something out, but we need proof."

"Kidding me, right? The wanker killed her himself. What the hell more proof do you need?"

"We need proof she's actually dead."

"I'm in the forest right now getting ready to put her in the ground and you want me to drive her stinking corpse back to the city? Forget it, mate. You can take your chances with the cops when I call them."

"A pic of the body," I tell him. "Or no deal."

The phone goes quiet.

"Alright," says the Jerk. "That's a go, but any more demands and your client will be hocking his story to Identification Discovery just to make bail. Give me a bit to get her out of the tarp. Where do I send it?"

I give him Trixie's number.

"Cheers," he says. The call goes dead.

Twenty minutes later, Trixie receives two pics. The first is a close up of Mrs. Brennan, a striking woman with blond hair and classic good looks, making reasonable allowances for the crescent-shaped gash across her forehead. The second is a wide-angle shot of her stretched out on the ground amid a cluster of trees.

"Okay…" Trixie cracks her knuckles, then pecks furiously at the screen on her cell.

"What are you doing?"

"Photo enhancement. Sharpening the image. Adjusting the contrast and…*cash money!* You owe me, baby."

"For what?"

"Solving the case." She slings the scarf around her neck and heads for the door. "Come on, Joe! I'll explain on the way."

Brennan has a dweeb-fit when Trixie hustles him out of the office and into his Lincoln Town Car, the three of us cramming in front with Trixie taking center seat to do what she does best.

"Hit it, Arthur. Burn some gas!"

"I don't understand why I have to drive." He squeals into traffic on Ridge Avenue. "Where are we going?"

"Straight. Then take Kelly Drive through Fairmount Park." Trixie elbows me, pointing to the close-up of Mrs. Brennan. "That gash on her forehead. Pretty clean, wouldn't you say?"

"So?"

"So where's the splatter? The blood that would have seeped from the wound? It's as if her face was wiped clean afterward."

"Is that my wife?" The Lincoln drifts into opposing traffic then jerks back in a blast of horns.

"Eyes on the road, Arthur! Turn here!"

The Lincoln cuts a wide arc on North Ferry through the clustered intersection under the bridge, scattering bikers in the Green Lane and sending the line at the hot dog cart lunging for cover before careening in a screech of rubber southbound onto Kelly Drive.

I clutch the door handle when the Lincoln hits seventy-five, switching lanes wildly as the road S-curves along the river through the park.

"But this is the real kicker." She zooms in on Mrs. Brennan's forehead, glistening with sweat.

"Alright," I say, both hands on the door handle with Kung Fu grip. "So she's sweating. Big deal. Got to be ninety degrees out here. Probably even hotter in Jersey. Can you ease up a bit, Artie?"

"Arthur," scolds Trixie, "you keep your tiny-little munchkin feet on the fuckin' gas!" She shoots me a quizzical look. "I'm surprised at you, Joe. Dead bodies don't sweat."

Hugging the curb on the straightaways, the Lincoln swings wide into opposing traffic at every curve. Horns blasting us on the left. The blur of oak trees on the right.

"By the way, Arthur?" says Trixie.

"Huh?" Brennan is white-knuckling the steering wheel. Riding on fear.

"By any chance did you make that lovely bride of yours sign a pre-nuptial agreement?"

"Had to. My first wife really took me to the cleaners."

"Cash money," Trixie laughs, giving me one of her looks. "Explains why the divorce plan wouldn't work. And check this out." She flips to the wide-angle of Mrs. Brennan lying on the ground and zooms in on the background. Barely visible through the trees is the outline of a familiar figure. "You see that?"

It's fuzzy at that magnification, but I can make out the shape of a man in a billowing cape with a walking stick and pilgrim's hat. Seen it before, but the threat of impending death has me unable to recall where.

"I'll be damned!" Brennan swerves the Lincoln across the center line, through a split-second window of opportunity between a Chevy Tahoe and what has to be the last running Suzuki Samurai on the planet. We hit the breakdown lane on the other side doing sixty and skid thirty yards through the gravel before coming to a cockeyed, dust-cloud stop behind a '90s-era Crown Vic. "That's the car! The clunker that was in my driveway when I went back to the house!"

In a clearing in the woods on the other side of the Vic stands a bronze statue of a pilgrim with a billowing cape and a walking stick. Must've passed it a million times.

I pry my hands off the door handle. "Nice work, Trix!"

The Jerk emerges from the woods with Brennan's very-much-alive wife. Brennan is out of the Lincoln and on top of them before they see him coming. He executes an uncoordinated right hook and the Jerk goes down without protest, spread-eagled in the dirt.

"You go, Arthur!" Trixie cackles.

"Artie!" Mrs. Brennan screams.

"Conniving little wench!"

"What about you? Leaving me for dead!"

"You're not dead!"

"Jackass!"

"Slut!"

She launches at Brennan and makes quick work of wrestling him into a headlock, the two of them spinning in circles as she knees him in the skull.

Trixie and I step out of the Lincoln and take a moment to assess our options.

"So what I'm thinkin' is," I point to a hiking trail leading back the way we came, "probably a good idea we hoof it from here. Messy domestic scene like this? Don't wanna be around when the heat shows up."

"Too late."

A police cruiser skids to a stop in the gravel behind us. The doors fly open and both cops laser in on the happy couple.

"Break it up you two!"

Strolling down the trail, I glance over my shoulder to where Brennan is taking a few final licks as they pry the little missus away. "So, whadaya think? We owe the guy a partial refund? I mean, that was pretty quick work."

"I dunno," Trixie chuckles. "Let's see if he asks."

"You know, Trix, it's a tough grind. The long hours. The demanding clients. But when a case like this comes along and everything works out in the end? Makes me feel like we're doing… I dunno, like we're doing—"

"God's work, Joe." She unloosens her scarf and slings an arm over my shoulder. "Like we're doing God's work."

Canary

by Matthew J. Hockey

Booster cleared the mist off his respirator goggles and pressed his face to the mail slot of 222 Foxglove Avenue.

Even through the mask, the air tasted of rotten fish and garlic that had fallen way down in a trash compactor. The living room was dark; the blinds drawn, sprayed-black bubble wrap taped over the glass. He had to wait until the television cut to an overlit game show before he could see what he was looking at.

A big pair of feet planked rigor mortis-stiff off the end of the sofa, twisted at an angle that was just wrong. The socks were too small and had individual rainbow-colored toes. Cute. God, he hoped it was a man wearing his girlfriend's socks. The women were always the worst.

The second vic had collapsed in the corner, toppling his chair as he did and spilling marshmallow cereal all over the floor. The milk and bloody vomit were still beaded on the carpet. He was a small Latino guy, wiry and shirtless to show off his ink and the tangle of chains around his neck. The St. Christopher winked in the dark.

The coffee table had a set of heavy-duty digital scales and there were empty glass containers all over the room—jugs, bottles, dishes, glasses, tumblers and even a tipped-out flower vase.

He slapped the slot down and turned back to the rest of the fire crew. They hung back by the truck, decked in full turnout gear and helmets, masks hanging down by their chests, axes and flatheads in hand ready to take the door. Police had closed off the cul-de-sac with sawhorses and cruisers parked side-on. Twice they'd had to call for additional reinforcements to contain the crowds—ghouls, local media types, looky-loos and honest-to-goodness residents who'd been evacuated from their homes and wanted nothing more than to see their neighbor's house go up with a bang.

"Don't leave me in suspense here," Delroy, the incident commander, said. His mutton chops were already slicked with sweat. Small Nevada towns weren't supposed to get this exciting.

"Two down."

Delroy waved the site runner over.

"Get dispatch to send another bus. The John Q that called it in missed one," he said before turning back to Booster. "What do you think? Carb Mox?"

"No. Whatever it is, it took them fast. They were dead before they had a chance to get sleepy."

"The boiler vents are taped off and there's extra thick insulation on the roof. We think cook lab."

"That gels with what I saw. This could be really bad. If they were using hypo acid instead of red phosphorus and they got it too hot…well, then we've got ourselves a house full of phosphine. Not only will it turn your lungs to cat food, it self-ignites in air. If we try and vertical vent it, it'll oxidize."

"Shit. Could anybody still be alive in that?"

"I don't know."

"You're the one with the chemistry degree."

"Maybe."

"I'll get the boys to draw straws. See who gets to be the canary."

"Screw that," Booster said, "I'll do it. And forget your two-in two-out. If it goes, it goes. It won't matter how many are in there if it does."

Delroy gave him an 'attaboy' pat on the ass. They'd both known he was going to say that. The rest of the crew wolf-whistled.

Booster pre-planned his moves with the site safety officer while Delroy spread the word that all firemen hate: HAZMAT call. Four more engines and a decontamination unit headed in from the next county over. The police pushed the hot zone perimeter out to three hundred and fifty feet. A local church group shuttled the neighbors to City Hall to sleep on mats and bitch about not being allowed back into their homes.

Ungrateful assholes, Booster thought as he stepped up to the door. He saves them from a choking death in their beds and they complain they didn't have time to pack an overnight bag.

He ran a last check on his gear, cinched his sleeve and ankle cuffs, and made sure there was no exposed skin. He fitted the pry into the door. His blood boiled in his face, his visor misted over again. His lungs pinched and his breath Darth Vadered in his ears. His ass was tight enough to snap pencils. If it was going to go off, it would go off when he opened the door—that first rush of air like the house inhaling and then… *crump*. He slammed his weight on the pry and the door popped.

One. Two. No explosion. So far so very, very good.

"I'm in," he said into the helmet radio.

"Keep it coming," Delroy said.

He marked the quickest route between exit and entry in case he had to exfil in a hurry. He checked upstairs first. If there were survivors that's where they'd be, Phosphine being heavier than air.

Upstairs was empty. No furniture except for a couple sleeping bags and a camping bed. Small plastic barrels of stuff with NFPA hazard diamonds on them. He checked them all close. If something was going to detonate, he wanted to know about it before it did. Just as he suspected—hypophosphorous acid. He was amazed it had taken them this long to kill themselves, they'd been so sloppy with the empties.

"Second floor clear, no casualties."

He went back downstairs to the living room, forced himself to look at victim one on the sofa. It was a man. A large white guy in his late twenties with dirty-looking dreadlocks and blood all around his nose. His neck cords had popped out when he'd been fighting for air. His eyes were open, covered in a thin layer of dust. He must have been pretty out of it on something not to try and escape.

Same for victim two by the radiator. No lividity. No discoloration. Bloody milk all over his chest. Gang tats and girls' names over his collarbone, Portuguese words instead of eyebrows. He had the teeth of a three-year meth user, lips pulled up in a snarl.

Booster pushed through a bead curtain into the boxy kitchen. Victims three, four and five lay at his feet. Three cats bunched together by the taped-up cat flap, tufts of fur lay all around them where they'd torn at each other in their panic.

He opened the door at the end of the room and found victim six collapsed halfway down the stairs to the basement. He had long bleached hair pulled into a ponytail that had flicked forward over his face, the sort of strands he would have blown away if his lungs still worked. He was half into a white chemical suit like crime scene techs wear. He'd been pulling it on as he went up the stairs, except it tangled it around his feet and he fell. It wouldn't have done him any good, the ratty old thing was full of cigarette holes.

It was a cook lab alright, a big one too. They'd set up two rows of tables covered with equipment; plastic and glass tubing ran between three liter milk bottles, the liquid inside had split into two distinct layers. A camp stove was set beneath a paint can—it was blackened from where the powder had burned. Good thing the flame had died before the phosphine got any denser. It would have taken the whole building with it when it went.

Booster was having to work too hard to drag in air. The fog on his Perspex wouldn't wipe away. His shins brushed against something as he made for the stairs back up. *Don't look*, he thought, *keep going, get outside.*

Instead he stopped. He bent down. He looked.

"Holy fucking shit," he said.

Delroy chirped in his ear. "What's going on? Are you ok? Say something?"

"It's mo…it's nothing. I fell off a step."

It wasn't nothing. It was a long way from nothing. It was a canvas gym bag stuffed with brown dust-covered money. Fat stacks of it wrapped around with hair scrunchies and jammed into pairs of ladies' tights. Too much to count.

"Boost. We're getting antsy. How's it going?"

"There's a third casualty in the basement."

He didn't know why he did it. He was on a good wage. His wife Cassie earned the same as him and then a third as much again. Plus her dad was loaded and she was his favorite, smack dab at the top of the inheritance tree. The mortgage was paid off. He didn't have children to take care of and no chance of any coming along. He didn't have any credit cards or overdrafts to worry about, student debts were all paid off. He didn't have…

He zipped the bag closed, wrapped it five times around with trash bags and dumped it in the open top of the water tank. He went back up to the kitchen. He was about to step through into the living room when…

…slap…

Sounded like a landed fish flopping on deck.

Victim Two. The gangbanger. He jerked from the waist and tried to sit up, fell back with another slap. He gagged and spat up red froth at the corner of his mouth, both hands to his throat and his eyes rolling in fright. Very much awake. Very much afraid. He held out his hands as best he could.

Booster bent down to him. He was about to pull him into a lift and get him out to the ambo when he stopped.

He didn't think about doing it, he just did it. It wasn't until later on that he tried to rationalize it. He lifted the cushion from under Victim One's rainbow socks. He pressed it over the gangbanger's face and jammed a knee into his chest. He didn't have to apply much pressure, just enough to feel the shape of the nose pressing into the fabric. The gangbanger didn't struggle much, he was ninety percent checked-out anyway.

He timed a minute and a half on his watch and then put the cushion back under the first guy's head. He went outside to the decontamination truck and let the chemical boys do their work.

By the time he got home, his dinner was in the microwave; a heart-stopper slab of Cassie's homemade lasagna squeezed into a Perry's ice-cream tub. She'd even put a freshly cut sprig of rosemary on the top to show him there were no hard feelings. She was a rare find that way, a fireman's wife that said 'I understand we won't get to see much of each other,' and actually still meant it ten years after the fact.

He heated it and slapped the pasta on two slices of floury white bread; a big carb crash was the only way he was going to sleep. He pulled a seat up to the kitchen island and ate the loose ground beef with a spoon.

Arms wrapped around his neck.

His skin went cold, his hairs stood on end, the chunk of burning onion stuck in his throat.

They've found me.

The hands moved on down to his chest and pinched. Cassie. He carried on chewing, and she pulled up another stool. She told him all about her day at the flower show; the flash of inspiration she'd had, the awesome rockery she'd seen. She told him how her work diary was looking for the next month—two landscaping consultations next week, another two the week after. When she'd first set up shop, she'd barely been making two consultations a quarter.

"I tell you I don't know how I'm going to fit it all in. Remember we didn't know how it was going to work out when I first quit Teller's? Now me, Cassiopeia Brewster *nee* Du Grange, a little girl from Caliente, is in a position to actually turn work down. Paying work. Can you imagine? Baby we might be able to get that pool after all…one with bubble jets!"

Her mouth kept moving. He knew he should be listening, should probably be responding. As it was, he couldn't even summon a *uh-huh* or a solitary *oh yeah* with any conviction. He felt that nose poking into the palm of his hand.

"I can get rid of the Ford if Mr. Shellacky comes through, get the Lexus I've had my eye on. Every day I go past Egan's, I check if it's still in the lot. I know I shouldn't, somebody's bound to have bought it by then but…anyway, Shellacky's a shoe-in. The man has koi carp. They don't come cheap. If he bites, that's sixty thousand dollars plus materials. I'd need to get in some laborers out of that, but still… Three months work! Where should we go on vacation? I was thinking South America. It should be coming up to Carnival time. Mardis Gras. Get some of the Latino spice… "

He slapped his hand palm-down on the countertop.

Cassie's mouth snapped shut. She tucked her chair in neatly and went to bed. He ate one, two, three more spoons of lasagna. The bedroom door slammed. The bed springs groaned. He threw the bowl at the wall—it bounced off and sprayed orange sauce all over the room. He spent half an hour mopping it up and went to bed himself. The carbs didn't help him sleep, they just gave him indigestion.

Two weeks later, the county fire examiner had finished his report, the chief medical examiner had released the bodies to whatever family the three bastards had, and even the Narco-squad boys had finished picking over the bones. Not a one of them had reported finding any money, but then why would they? Booster knew he should feel like he was in the clear, but he didn't. He felt like he had a lump in his lungs that he couldn't cough up.

He took a personal day, the first one he'd taken since his dad's diagnosis fifteen years ago. Delroy didn't even ask what it was for, just nodded and said, "Don't worry about it. Take as long as you want."

He parked two blocks over from the cookhouse and walked. Nobody had thought to replace the door and it swung inward with a gentle push. Snagged ends of crime scene tape littered the floor and it seemed like every surface was spread with print-lifting powder. The carpets had been pulled up to show the bare wood and the paper had been stripped off the walls. He had to force himself to breathe, convinced that if he did, he'd start vomiting blood.

There was a tall fat man in blue coveralls in the living room standing on the exact spot where the Latino had died. He had wild tufts of white hair spraying out of either side of his head and his bald dome was knotted with blue veins. He ran a black box over the wall. It pipped over a section of blank plaster and a red LED shone. He drew a pencil mark, clipped ear-defenders to his head, and fitted a two-handed drill to the spot. He pulled the trigger and it shrilled into motion. He bored a hole in seconds, right down to the support stud. It was loud enough to make Booster hold his ears and cry out.

The fat man took his finger off the drill trigger and waited for it to run down before he turned.

"Who might you be?" He spoke like his jaw was wired.

"Jack Brewster. I'm with the fire department."

"Vince Marshall. I do electrics." He pushed a long hooked tool into the hole in the wall and fished out a tube of white plastic and wire. "They told me you all was finished. I'll be right out of your hair."

"It's okay."

"Nah don't worry about it." He opened his toolkit and tucked the thing into a compartment with a half-dozen identical pieces of white plastic and wires. "I'm near enough sewed-up here anyway." He lifted his case and went outside. Booster watched him all the way into his van. It went down on its axels when he climbed in. He opened a newspaper on his lap and pulled a half-eaten hoagie off the dash.

Booster went through to the kitchen and opened the door to the basement. It still smelled of fish and garlic down there. The bottom three steps had dark stains, one of them had a handprint right in the center. He rolled his sleeves up and plunged his arms to the bottom of the water tank. He touched metal.

It was gone…

…jerked his hands around and..

…it's gone…

…felt plastic crinkle under his nails. He yanked it back out and tore it open, threw the shreds into the water. The bag had a few wet patches, nothing too major. He hefted it onto his shoulder and made his way out. It was heavier than he remembered.

Halfway up the stairs, he noticed another hole drilled into the grey cinderblock wall, two more in the kitchen, another he hadn't spotted in the living room. Vince's van wasn't outside. He'd left his drill plugged into the jack.

He tried not to run back to his car, tried to keep his steps slow and measured. He made it all of a hundred yards before he gave in and sprinted.

Four thousand and sixteen crisp green notes.

Was it worth what he'd done?

He spread them all over his laundry room floor, looking for one that wasn't a hundred. He spent two hours. He didn't find one. He was so freaked he had to use a calculator to work out how much it was. That made it even worse. More real. He had to type it in ten times before he'd believe it.

Four hundred and one thousand, six hundred dollars.

It was worth it.

He didn't leave a note. Didn't even plan on leaving. He was on his way to the Chevron station to fill the tank for the weekend, maybe pick up a six-pack of Heineken, when all of a sudden it was five hours later and he was on US 395 northbound into Reno.

He kept to the outer edge of the city, well away from the tourist traps and the pro gamblers, anybody that would make him as an out-of-town mark. He pulled into the lot of a down-at-the-heels casino. He'd heard of the Grand Sierra, the Atlantis, Harrah's, the Peppermill and all the others. But this…well, this wasn't that. The Zephyr was the sort of place people came if they had been blackballed from the real casinos or had nothing else pressing to do with the last days of their terminal illness. There was a girl out front directing people where to park, even though there were only four other cars in the lot.

He took his bag out of the trunk and kicked it across the floor like it held nothing but dirty laundry, got it good and scuffed with dust. He scooped it up and made his way to the joint reception/cash desk.

Two out of the casino's three bars were closed down and shuttered. Most of the gaming tables were covered over with maroon dropcloths. A sea of silver hair and sunburned bald spots pecked away at the slot machines.

There was a wall of coin-op lockers painted with gold glitter by the elevators, somewhere for the guests to stash their bags where they could still see them from the floor. He fed a few coins into one of the lockers, slid the bag in and kicked it home. He took out sixteen hundred and left the rest.

He drove to a real casino, to check into a room—one with a name Cassie would recognize. Halfway there, he wrenched the fob off the locker key and tossed it out of the window just in case some punk rolled him.

He'd planned on playing the sixteen hundred out over three days—he lost it in forty-six minutes. Roulette, blackjack and poker took the lion's share and the slots gobbled up the rest. It felt surreal, throwing it all away and being happy about it. He'd have been glad enough to win, but it wasn't necessary for the plan. He'd only come to get the receipt when he cashed the money into chips; it had the casino's name splashed across the top of the strip.

He was going to show up home with the bag and the receipt. He could see it now:

"I have no idea what came over me. I just felt lucky. I put it all on your birthday. I told myself I'd stop as soon as I stopped winning. Well baby... I didn't stop winning."

He'd put the bag on the table so they could count it together. They'd fuck on it, and then they'd go out to the garage and that white Lexus would be there...and if they weren't too tired, they'd fuck in there too. If he kept the story coming quick enough to keep her on her back foot, she probably wouldn't ask questions.

Now he just needed to hang loose and wait for enough time to pass that she'd buy it. Three days should do it. Three days and a phone call. He'd tell her about the bodies, how it had bothered him more than usual, just needed some time to himself is all.

He went up to his room and chained the door behind him, lay his head against the wood and sighed. Hands came down around his neck.

Not Cassie's.

They spun him into the wall hard enough to knock the picture off its hook, then pulled a sock around his face and up into his mouth. He gagged and tried to get ahold of their arms, push off the door frame and slam his attackers to the ground. Something pressed into his back. He didn't have to see it to know what it was. He put his hands up and let himself be led over by the bed.

Two men sat in the armchairs by the window. One looked to be in his sixties with huge forward-tilting glasses. They shone white with reflected sunlight and obliterated his face. He had the air of a kindly grandfather. His fingers were covered in loose silver rings that he purposefully jangled together as he folded his hands on his crossed legs. He nodded to the chair that had been turned to face them and the big guy behind Booster pushed him into it.

"Who..?" Was all he got out before the sock pressed his tongue flat.

"My name is Elvis," the old man said.

"Look, I just lost all my money downstairs. I might have a fifty in my jeans..." Booster said. The big guy yanked the sock again.

"Show him Ry," Elvis said to the man beside him.

Ry was a lot younger, sporting a hipster beard, suspenders over a Breton sweater and a wool cap that looked like a reservoir-tip condom. He reached down into the Herschel bag between his legs and drew out a laptop.

His arms were thick and muscled, though they looked to have been earned from working, rather than three hours a day at the gym.

He flipped the laptop around on his knees and pressed a few keys. A video spooled up. It was full color, high up on the wall of Foxglove Avenue. It showed the two dead guys.

Booster looked up. Vince the electrician smiled down at him, grabbed him around the cheeks and turned his head back to watch. They made him watch himself murder the kid on the floor.

They made him watch it again.

They made him watch it again.

He cracked on the third run-through. He sobbed. He blew snot all over his lips.

"He was eighteen years old. Anybody tell you that?" Elvis asked, he didn't wait for Booster to answer. "Where's my money?"

"When I went back for it, it was gone."

Vince pulled back even harder on the sock and pinned him in the chair. Elvis pushed Booster's legs apart with his own knees and drew a lock-knife as though he was just clicking his fingers. He pressed the tip to Booster's balls and leaned into his face, his breath smelled of new leather. "Where is my money?"

"Maybe the Narc boys found it."

Elvis pressed the knife tip harder into Booster's crotch. "Last chance. Where is my money?"

"Go fuck yourself!" Even Booster was surprised when he said it.

Elvis looked into his eyes. Booster didn't blink, sure that if he did, he was dead.

"We can't do him here boss." Ry tugged on Elvis's sleeve like a little boy trying to get his father's attention.

"Bring the car around." Elvis snapped the knife closed.

They took the elevator and walked him out through the lobby to the parking lot like they were old pals going to catch a floorshow. They let him ride up front just long enough to drive out to an abandoned lot and then they hustled him into the trunk of a waiting black Lincoln Continental.

They took his phone, his keys and his wallet. They didn't tie his hands but there was nothing in the trunk to defend himself with, no jack, no tire iron, nothing. He tried to memorize the turns; two lefts, one right, straight on ten minutes. He lost track. His mind and his heart raced and he couldn't keep it straight. It was hot in there, choking, loose gravel and stones pinged off the metal.

They drove for two hours over rough ground. His muscles cramped and his head ached from bouncing off the bodywork. He'd decided to tell them, to tell them everything. It was the only way he was getting out.

The car slewed to a stop and feet crunched over the ground toward him. They popped the lid and he had to force his eyes to open. The sky was still light and the three men were nothing but black shapes against it. They pulled him out and set him on his feet. One of them kicked him in the ass and he stumbled away from them into a stand of sickly creosote.

They were out in the high desert, surrounded by dark shapes of the mountains and screening walls of dust blown by the wind howling through the cracks. The ground was soft and their footprints were crisscrossed with animal tracks.

"Dig." Elvis threw a tooth-edged military shovel on the ground in front of him. Vince aimed along the iron-sights of an AK-47 decked out in zebra print like an African warlord's assault rifle. Ry had a pair of pearl-handled revolvers tucked into his shorts.

"I'll tell you anything you want to know." Booster bent to pick up the shovel.

"That time's gone. We'll find it the old-fashioned way. Now dig."

"Where?"

"Down."

Booster picked a spot out by the rocks and swung the shovel. It bit in easily. His sweat ran. His back screamed. The wind whipped the loose dirt in wide fans that stung his eyes. His plan was to throw the shovel at anybody who strayed close enough, get their gun and make for the car. Except none of them moved. Elvis smoked by the Lincoln and made calls on his cell. Ry sat on a rock and drew patterns in the sand with a stick. Vince's arm got tired and the AK hung from his shoulder by a strap. He noticed Booster looking and motioned him back to digging.

The hole got big enough to step down into. They shushed him whenever he tried to speak. They weren't going to kill him though. No way. They were going to make sure he was good and scared and then ask him again where the money was. He'd tell them the moment they let him. Drive them right to it if they wanted. He'd had his fun. They'd call a halt soon. No doubt. Any minute now.

Except he kept digging and digging and the sun hit the downslopes and he kept right on digging until he was up to his thighs. His mouth was dry as brushwood and his palms were blistered and bloody from the shovel handle.

"Stop." Vince came to the side of the hole, though he stayed just out of range.

"Wait wait wait…" Booster carried on digging, chipping away at the rocks, throwing up sparks.

"If boss says it's deep enough, it's deep enough." He kicked stones in with the edge of his boot, spackling them across the back of Booster's head.

He carried on, frantic now, just one more shovelful, just one more. He clipped the red rocks by the edge of the hole and stones rattled way down into the cracks.

"Hurry it up!" Ry yelled.

"You want to do it, pissmop?" Vince called back over his shoulder. The stones were still rattling in the rock, sounding like a tambourine made out of bones. Booster realized what it was a second before Vince. He snapped and reached into the crack to grab it. His hand closed around something sinewy and strong, he threw it before he knew what he was doing.

The rattlesnake hit Vince in the chest. He squealed and stomped his feet, overbalanced and pitched into the hole. Ry drew one of his pistols and fired, the bullet buzzing overhead. Booster grabbed the shovel and smashed it into Vince's teeth. He gagged as the biting edge hit the roof of his mouth and wrapped his hands around the back of Booster's leg. Another bullet whistled by and thumped into the dirt. Booster lifted his foot and stomped on the head of the shovel. It cut through Vince's jaw to the dirt below. Black blood welled up in his nose and eyes.

Booster stomped once more with a roar of effort and lifted the AK. Ry was running toward him as he burst up out of the ground. Ry's eyes went wide as he saw the gun. He fell over trying to turn as Booster fired. The rifle butt kicked him so hard, he fell backwards and sprayed bullets into the car door. The alarm went off.

Urr-urr urr-urr urr-urr

Ry's footsteps crunched across the hardpack. Booster pulled himself up. Propped the gun solidly against himself and squeezed off one round. Ry's calf exploded in a red gout, and he toppled screaming into the bushes.

Urr-urr urr-urr urr-urr

Booster closed him down and put a spray into his back. One of his suspenders snapped and flicked back hard enough to whip his ass. Booster rolled him over with his foot—his eyes were half-lidded and his tongue stretched down onto his chin with a wet bubble of saliva.

Urr-urr urr-urr urr-urr

The bullet hit Booster before he heard the shot. It went into his guts and ripped out of his back. He felt a hot, wet lump tented against the inside of his shirt. He fell to his knees and the next one hit him in the ribs. It burned inside. His heart skipped a beat. Then another. Then another.

Urr-urr urr-urr urr-urr

Then another. The next beat shuddered through his shattered bones. He howled and spun. Elvis leaned over the hood of the car, both hands wrapped around a flat-grey automatic. Booster fired until the gun clacked dry. The car disappeared in a cloud of black dust and paint chips. He rolled to Ry's body and tore the revolver out of his hand.

He dragged himself around the trunk of the car and found Elvis crouched in the dirt. His legs were a patchwork of blood and bone flakes. His gun was three feet away. He had a wallet clutched in his hand. He flipped it open as Booster came up on him. It had a gold eagle DEA badge.

"Don't," he said. "I'll make it worth…"

Booster put the revolver to his head and fired. His forehead collapsed in on itself. Booster frisked him for the car keys and got in. His stuff was in the bag in the footwell. He found his phone and called Cassie.

It went through to voicemail.

"I love you Cassie. I just wanted you to know that. I love you so much. I don't know how much time I have. I tried to do something, I'm not going to lie to you and tell you it was for us. It was just something I did and now it's done and I'm dying. I'm going to try and get somewhere where somebody will find my body. If I do, when they release my stuff to you, there'll be a key you don't recognize. Don't say anything. It belongs to locker four-oh-three in the Zephyr hotel in Reno. There's a present in there for you. I love you. I love you. I love you."

He wasn't sure how much of it recorded before the second beep cut him off. He wasn't sure if the car would start with all the bullet holes in the hood. He wasn't sure where he was going since the wind had destroyed the tracks.

He turned the key in the ignition.

The Fair

by Dan J. Fiore

FOREST HILLS POLICE DEPARTMENT
CASE FILE: FH.347.007.94 (See also: FH.347.007.89)
INTERVIEWER: Detective Damon Gruski
INTERVIEWEE: Gale Bram (Hough)
DATE: 10/25/2014

[Tape's beginning is cut off.]...might've already heard this from Marcy, but when I visited her in the hospital yesterday she told me that, while she was watching the neighborhood kids at the fair play around the merry-go-round, she'd seen something no one else could see.

Did she tell you this already?

We haven't been able to speak with Mrs. Melfi yet, no. The doctors...

Oh, well, she was in her booth. "The children glowed in the bright daylight," she said. "The tiny patter of their sneakers on the playground pavement blotted out all the noise. The buzzers. The bells. The music, laughter and conversation." She told me that what she saw in the kids' shadows running alongside them, it calmed this—"frigid quiver," I think is how she put it—this frigid quiver that had been locked in her ribcage for days.

This...*thing*, it mimicked their movements and clung to their heels. And when she recognized it for what it was, she felt a warmth spread through her cheeks, through her stomach and her heart. Even just laying there, strapped to her bed and describing it to me, that fog behind her eyes—you know what I mean? Well, that fog lifted, and a smile sort of teased the corners of her lips. All because of what she said waited there in the darkness following the children.

What was it?

Her son.

Let's just—let's stick with your own version of the events, Mrs. Bra—

Miss Hough, please. Or just Gale's fine, too.

Miss Hough. Okay, go ahead.

Well, it was an accident, what happened. Of course. I want that on the record.

Just one text and this brief blur crossing in front of me. That's all it took. **[Hough snaps her fingers.]** Barely a blink of distraction. And maybe I guess a little too much wine, but I don't think that played too big of a part considering how fast everything happened.

I told myself over and over, like it mattered, *It was just an accident.* Like that would help. As if that made any difference.

I'm sorry. Hold on. Sorry. **[Hough digs a tissue from her pocket, blows her nose, wipes her eyes.]** Sorry. Anyway, so yeah… I kept repeating this in my head like some kind of meditation mantra. I'd remind myself again and again to just focus on Jason. *Think about Jason.* You know? Like I was doing yoga or something. But still, against every instinct screaming through my body, I followed Father Richard into the back of that booth.

Mrs. Melfi's booth.

Yes. Well, it was at that point. It was supposed to be Mrs. Porbansky's booth, to sell her haluski. But I guess Marcy kicked her out.

"Been my spot the past four years," she told Father.

What was your initial impression of Mrs. Melfi that afternoon? What sort of state was she in?

She was a mess. I mean, she looked littler. Frail. Her hair had lost almost all of its color, and she was the kind of woman who, despite her age, never let a gray root show. Vigilant with the brown hair dye, for sure. I think she always felt uncomfortable being so much older than the other mothers in the neighborhood.

And she *really* never looked older than she did on the day of the fair.

That's no judgment on her part. Obviously, you know, anyone would look ancient going through what she was going through—what she's *still* going through and will most likely never stop having to go through. But I mean, she looked…scary. Skin pale. Eyes dull. Oh, her eyes. Her one eye—I'm sure you saw it—it was like half closed all of a sudden. Just hanging in this half-blink. **[Hough shivers.]** It was never like that before. Just watching her stand there talking to Father, this wicked feeling bloomed in my belly. Like some kind of….poisonous flower or something.

I knew something wasn't right.

What was Father Richard talking to Mrs. Melfi about?

Just that, you know, she shouldn't be there. He was worried. I think everyone was worried. Father Richard was just the only one who would do something about it.

And apparently yourself.

Well, I mean, guilt makes you do a lot of things you wouldn't normally do, I guess. But, yeah, Father stood there talking to her while she handed out baskets of her rigatoni. I could only barely hear most of what he said because he was trying to whisper. But he mentioned her husband, how she should be home with him. He said something about this being too soon or too early or something, which I definitely agreed with. He even scolded her for not coming up for communion at mass that morning.

"Faith can be a powerful weapon in times like this," I think he said.

Marcy just quietly nodded. Kept handing out pasta.

There was this teenager. A high school kid from down on Winterburn. He was kind of rude I guess, and Marcy made him say "please" like three or four times before she let him have any.

Still didn't charge him though.

And you didn't find it odd she wasn't charging people?

Maybe a little. That was the first I'd—

[Hough holds up a finger and gags, spits twice into the waste bin provided. Hough pauses before she wipes her mouth and continues.] Sorry. But I didn't really think much of it. When I'd dropped off a casserole at her house a few days earlier, she'd told me she was thinking of making her rigatoni for the fair. She said rigatoni was always Michael's favorite. *Iganoni*, she said he used to call it.

I thought maybe this was just her way of grieving. Or, I don't know, something.

You visited Mrs. Melfi's house before the fair?

[Hough nods.] Two days before, I think. Friday? She seemed in rough shape then, but nowhere near as bad as Sunday.

What else did you two talk about Friday?

Nothing much. I mean, she wasn't very talkative. Her husband, Bud, was drinking down in the basement. I could hear home movies, really loud, coming up through the kitchen floor.

But Marcy and me, we were never really close to begin with. I just stopped by to drop off some food and check to see if maybe there were any new developments in the case. If they suspected me at all yet. I guess I actually ended up being the only one from the neighborhood who ever actually showed up.

And that's when you met Detective Chauncey?

On my way out, yes, he was just pulling up.

The day of the fair, you remained in Mrs. Melfi's booth that whole afternoon. Correct?

I did.

You didn't seem too interested in keeping your distance.

Well, I guess I just felt sorry for her. You know? I'd done this to this woman. I wanted to make sure she didn't—I don't know, have a breakdown or something. Hurt herself, or whatever. I wanted her to be okay. So I stayed there with her after Father left.

Did you discuss what happened to Michael?

In a way, yes. She kept murmuring to herself, when she wasn't humming the same song I didn't recognize over and over, *Could've been any of them.* I mean, it was weird. All around us were these happy people out in the sun, just having a blast. You know? Families winning prizes and eating cotton candy. Kids, mothers, grandparents—all smiling. But under this little canopy at the corner of the football field, there was Marcy and me. Talking around this awful thing that'd happened. This nightmare.

I remember this pregnant woman coming up to the booth. Caitlyn McCormack. Smiling this great big smile of hers, brighter than the sun as always. "The girls were telling me you make the best Italian," she said to Marcy. "And I just had to come see for myself."

Marcy didn't smile. She just kind of shrugged. She asked Caitlyn when she was due and Caitlyn held up three fingers.

"Three weeks," she said. She rolled her eyes. "Can't come quick enough."

And Marcy stiffened. Her one eye went wide. "Don't you dare rush a thing," she hissed. "Not even that."

The look on that poor girl's face…

That poor, poor girl. And the baby.

[Pause.]

Anyway, Marcy handed her a basket after she apologized. Caitlyn went for her purse, but Marcy stopped her. "No," she said. "No money. Just…" And then she froze. Her eyes locked on the girl's plump belly, their focus somewhere past the shirt draped over it. Like she was really staring at that baby inside. You know? "Just enjoy," she said.

That was when I noticed the stain on Marcy's sleeve.

Stain?

Like a sauce stain. I told her about it, but she didn't seem to care. Or maybe she didn't even hear me. She just kept watching the pregnant woman as she walked away, sat down at a picnic table and started eating.

That was a busy part of the day. Pretty soon, a father with two kids came up and Marcy gave them free rigatoni too. Then an older couple, around retirement age. A volunteer on break. The Parkers from the street behind Marcy's house. Alison from PTO. The Roslens stopped by. The MacDowels. The youngest of the Shilling girls. Frank. Salina. Another middle-aged woman from church. A group of out-of-towners. All them and even more, they all smiled, said thank you, and Marcy would watch with a shaky hand held to her lips as each—**[Hough clears her throat.]**—as each of them ate. Then she'd mumble to herself again every once in a while, *Could've been any of them.*

You never asked her what she meant by that?

Well, I thought it was pretty obvious what she meant by it. I didn't know what she had planned, obviously, but why wouldn't she be wondering who did this to her son? What mother wouldn't?

So, at this point she didn't suspect you at all.

She had to. At least on some level. She kept asking me questions.

"Where's your Honda, Gale?"

"Why's Jason not here, Gale?"

"When's that book club of yours, Gale? And where's it at again?"

Why did she ask about your book club?

Some of the mothers around the neighborhood put it together. We meet once a month and drink wine and pretend we actually read whatever smutty novel one of us picked. But the thing is, we have it on Wednesday nights.

The same night…

Yeah. And we have it on Bigelow, at Meredith Glengarry's house.

Please explain why that's important.

On my way to and from Bigelow, I take the back road past Marcy's house.

So she did know.

I guess so. Maybe not at first, but by the end of the fair I think she'd pretty much figured it out.

When did the police arrive?

Pretty close to the end of the fair. Everything was kind of shutting down at that point. The music was off. People were cleaning up their booths, breaking down the games. Then these two cars pulled into the lot up by the middle school. A black Ford and a patrol car with its lights off. Detective Chauncey got out of the Ford.

And you hadn't eaten any of her food by that point.

No. We were just sitting there. I told Marcy the police were there and asked if she thought they maybe finally found a suspect. I was nervous, but I guess a little part of me was relieved. As much as I didn't want to lose—

[Pause.]

As much as I didn't want to lose Jason, I kept thinking what it'd be like if I was in Marcy's position. If it were my boy…

She deserves the truth.

Bud too.

How did Marcy react when you mentioned the police?

She didn't even seem to hear me. I think she actually—yeah, she actually asked if my divorce was done yet. I told her no, that we were still sorting everything out. Then she said I was lucky.

I was kind of shocked by that. Not just because of what happened with Michael, but because there didn't seem to be *anything* lucky about me and Carl's relationship.

"Jason's too young to know what's happening." That's what she said, what she meant. Then she said not to worry. "Mothers always win these things." Meaning custody. Although, I guess we can't say *always*. Not now that I'm in here talking to you…

[Pause.]

I—I ended up asking her what she thought the police were there for. Again, she didn't answer. Instead she asked me what I think about when I go up for communion. At this point, my mind was really just going about a million directions. These random questions and comments just made it worse.

I told her I didn't know. That I guess I prayed.

She asked what I pray about.

I don't remember what exactly I said, but I remember she again changed the topic right away, asking if I'd ever heard of some tribe in Papua New Guinea. The Forbes tribe or something? Anyway, she said she and Bud went there with Father on a mission trip before Michael was born. "I passed them off as heathens at first," she said. "But, it's such a fascinating culture." Then, rolling right off that she asked me again if my divorce was finalized yet, like she'd completely erased from her memory what we'd talked about the past five minutes. She stood there and stared at me, waiting for an answer as she scratched at the sauce stain on her sleeve.

Is that when the police arrived at the booth?

No. Not yet. It took Detective Chauncey a while to make his way around the football field to find us. There were a lot of booths. Lots of people.

But a boy came up—Aiden Palmeri. Just this little, precious angel. Blonde hair and red, round cheeks. **[In a small, high-pitched voice.]** "Rigatoni, please, Mrs. Melfi?"

[Hough pauses, smiling until she again begins to gag, her eyes watering.] I'm sorry. Anyway. Sorry. But, um, Marcy stood there staring at the baskets. I'm not sure for how long, but long enough that Aiden gave me this confused look for a second. Finally, Marcy's head bobbed up and down and she handed the boy one of the paper baskets of rigatoni. She leaned down to come face-to-face with him. "You eat all that now," she said. "You're a growing boy. Need to eat good so you can be big and strong someday, live a long, happy life." She reached out and wrapped her hand around Aiden's boney arm. "Hear?"

Aiden held up a crumbled ball of money his mom or dad must've given him.

Marcy just shook her head. "Go play a game or something," she said. "Have some fun."

Aiden smiled, but when he stepped back Marcy's hand stayed where it was. His arm was locked in her fist.

I took a step forward, not sure what was happening or what exactly I should do. But before I could reach out or say anything Marcy loosened her grip and Aiden slid out. He was about to wander away when he stopped and asked with his brow furrowed, "Where's Michael, Mrs. Melfi?" Hearing him ask that—

[Hough pulls another tissue from her pocket and blows her nose.]

Hearing that, it hurt enough for me. I can't even begin to imagine what was going through Marcy's head. And Marcy, she just rested a hand on the table. "Oh," she said. "I think he's around here somewhere." Her voice was just a croaking whisper. We both watched as Aiden ran off. He stopped between the long row of booths. With that ball of money in his one hand and the pasta—that pasta in the other, he stood staring at all the game tables still open.

[Hough takes in a deep, shaky breath.]

All the overwhelming possibilities before him.

[Pause.]

Do you need a break, Miss Hough?

No. No, I'm fine. Thank you. I'm sorry. I just—Where was I?

Oh, after, um—after Aiden left, a...uh, a balloon popped or something a few booths down. Loud and sudden, reaching out across the football field until another sound filled its place—this shrill, shattering scream. It took me a second to really realize what was happening.

Marcy was huddled on the ground at my feet, covering her head as she screamed over and over into the grass beneath her. I bent down and wrapped her in my arms, rocked her like I do Jason when he's having an episode. I kept telling her as her screams faded that it was okay, she was going to be okay.

It took her a few good minutes before she looked up at me, her face just a total wreck.

"You know that's true," I said to her. "Don't you? What you said to Aiden?"

She didn't seem to recognize me, those dull eyes of hers staring into mine. "Michael is still here, still looking down on you. He always will be."

Marcy didn't even blink.

"You should feel blessed," I said, "for the time you had with him."

Finally, she turned to the children playing by the swings. "Blessed?" she repeated.

I nodded. "Of course."

People all over our side of the fair stood staring at us on the ground. None of them made any move toward us.

"I remember sitting in the hospital bed. Holding him. His little fingers wrapped around one of mine. I knew I didn't deserve him, Gale. That I was too old and I'd been too selfish all my life to deserve such a glorious gift like him. First time in my life I thanked God. First time. I felt so blessed then. So blessed."

One-by-one the others around the booth went back to whatever they were doing.

I was crying now. Sobbing. Just completely lost in that guilt tearing me apart.

"I just want him to have the life he should've had," Marcy said. She looked at me again. "What mother wouldn't?"

I tried telling her then. Tried saying everything I promised myself I would never say to anyone. So I—so I wouldn't lose my son. So I wouldn't lose my Jason.

Tried?

Marcy wouldn't let me. She stood and every time I opened my mouth, got the start of what I wanted to say—what I *needed* to say—out, she shut me up. "It was an accident," she said. "There's no changing what happened."

I stood too.

"It was fate," she said. "That's all accidents are: God's plan in disguise. God wanted this to happen to my boy and God needed to make someone do it." She waved a crooked finger around the field. "Could've been any of them." Her eyes lifted to me a moment, struggling to stay there before dropping to the table next to her. She grabbed a basket of rigatoni and shoved it in my hands. "He's dead, Gale. My Michael's dead. Stop talking," she said. "And just eat."

I didn't understand. I couldn't. I'd never…I mean, *never* forgive someone if they took my son—my only child—from me. You know? But Marcy… I guess I don't know if she really meant it or not now. It seemed like she did. I want to believe she meant it. I don't know why she did what she did, but I don't think—as strange as it might sound—I don't think there was any hate or anger in it. At least not toward me. I don't think she wanted to hurt anybody. What she said seemed to kind of convince me of that, especially now.

What she said?

"God's not the only one with a plan."

[Pause.]

That was when I noticed the three policemen coming down our row of booths. Father Richard led them. He walked with his hands in his pockets, with his head carried low. The officers and the detective with their backs straight, shoulders cocked. Unhurried in a weird way, but still alert.

I told Marcy they were heading toward our booth and she asked me if I knew what *communion* meant. I was too thrown to possibly find an answer so Marcy told me it comes from the Latin word *communis*. "Means *to share*," she said. "Same Latin word we get *community* from." She repeated the word. Community. "Like a tribe," she said.

I didn't say anything. I didn't know what to say. So I just kept eating.

"Detective Chauncey looks tired," Marcy said.

I told her that there had to be some sort of development. Why else would they be there?

And she said— **[Hough clears her throat.]**

She said the funeral home probably called them.

I asked why, but Marcy didn't seem to hear me. She just looked over to the playground, watched the kids running around. There were only a few left by that point.

"What you're supposed to be thinking about," she said, "is the gracious gift of Christ."

I stopped chewing, my mind stuttering.

Because I hadn't said anything, Marcy glanced over her shoulder at me. "At communion, I mean." Her eyes returned to the approaching police and Father Richard. Her hand scratched at that arm again, where I'd seen the sauce stain earlier. But now, the inside of the sleeve was a cluttered ladder of red. Erratic, blurry red lines, layered side-by-side from mid-forearm up her bicep almost to her armpit.

Dread built and bubbled in the pit of my stomach. I knew then that something was happening—something awful. I could feel it around me, like the world's turning had slowed.

"You know," Marcy said. "You were wrong before. What you said about Michael."

I didn't—I wasn't sure what she meant.

"Michael's not looking down on me," she said.

I lowered the fork in my hand back into my basket of rigatoni. I stared at her, hollow with that swelling heartache. "Mar," I started to say.

But Marcy just lifted a hand. "He's not looking down on me," she repeated. She waved vaguely to the surrounding booths, the people still moving about. "He's all around me now." Finally, something like a smile crept along her lips. Again, she looked at me. "He's even standing right in front of me." And then her eyes dropped to the rigatoni in my hands.

END OF TRANSCRIPT

The Kompanski Incident

by Joseph Rubas

I read somewhere last night that Krusher Kompanski's going to be inducted into the World Wrestling Entertainment Hall of Fame next September. The headline said something like: CONTROVERSIAL PRO WRESTLER NOMINATED. The article went on to talk about his life and the "suspicious circumstances surrounding his death."

Suspicious my ass.

There's no ambiguity about it; I shot the motherfucker in his fat, ugly head, and everyone who gives a damn knows it. It was front page news when it happened. It was 1985, after all, right in the middle of the 1980s wrestling boom, so of course a wrestler getting blown away by a booker backstage was big news. What happened beforehand was big news too.

Let me back it up. In 1973, I was twenty—a tall, lanky kid with evil eyes and genius-level street smarts. I dropped out of high school when I was sixteen to work for my uncle, Anthoney DeNocco. If that name sounds familiar to you, it should: He was a captain in the Los Angeles Crime Family. They called him Tony Knocks. In September '73, Tony bought out a wrestling promotion based in Barstow called the Mojave Wrestling Federation (MWF). It was a popular act, had thirty guys and its own arena. Hell, it even had a lucrative Saturday morning timeslot on TV.

The owner, a fat little guy named Bill Watkins, was a gambler though, and most the money his company made went on the table, if you know what I mean. Every couple weeks, he'd drive out to L.A. and place bets with Uncle Tony. More often than not, he lost. Uncle Tony was a patient guy, and whenever Watkins couldn't pay, Tony'd give him a pass. Finally, he called in his debt, and man, was it a debt. I can't remember the exact figure, but it was a lot. Watkins said he'd have to close down shop and file for bankruptcy and still not have enough.

So Tony cut him a deal. Hand over the MWF and he'd call it even.

Watkins obliged.

Anyway, after they signed the paperwork but before Uncle Tony went out to Barstow, he gave me a call, and we met in the back of this lounge he owned in Newport Beach. He was a tall guy, lean and mean, with graying black hair and hard, blue eyes.

"You're into that wrestling crap, ain't ya?" he asked.

I shrugged. "I guess." Though I didn't let on, I was a huge fan...or rather, had been growing up. My favorite was always Gorgeous George. Wore silky capes and had his valet spray perfume in the ring. Back in Jersey we had Garden State Wrestling in Trenton, which aired on Saturday nights. Sometimes, when the wind was right, we got wrestling from Albany.

Tony nodded. "Alright. Tell me about it."

"What do you want me to tell you?"

Tony shrugged. "Tell me everything."

Lucky for his goombah ass, I was the kinda fan who liked to know history and shit, so I read a lot of books. I began his history lesson telling him that pro wrestling in the US started in carnivals, and even today wrestling insiders use a lot of carnie lingo.

Wrestling broke away in the twenties or thereabouts, and every region had its own thing. I don't know if they do it anymore, but back then, it all operated on a territory system. You had the National Wrestling Association (NWA) as a governing body (then in the sixties, the

American Wrestling Alliance came along), and under them you had dozens and dozens of different promotions, or companies. Think WWE or TNA today.

Promoters (bosses) only worked small patches of the country. There was Jim Crockett in Virginia and the Carolinas, Georgia Championship Wresting in Georgia, Southwest Wrestling All-Stars in Texas, New Mexico, and Arizona. If a promoter tried to promote himself on someone else's territory, there'd be hell to pay. You know, it's funny, but the NWA might as well have been another mob family. They did sneaky, underhanded shit, you know? This guy from Tennessee messing around in Ohio? Send someone to rough him up. Things like that.

Anyway, the MWF was strictly a California thing. Like I said earlier, it was based in Barstow, but it traveled through the desert on occasion, putting on outdoor shows during the summer. Every once in a while, it made it as far west as San Diego, but that's pretty much it.

"You know a lot," Tony said.

I shrugged. "I read books."

Tony laughed. "Be here tomorrow. We're goin to Barstow."

The next day, I met Tony at his place around eight, and we set off east on I-15 surrounded by hardscrabble flats tapering off to low, rugged mountains, Barstow's a lot like Vegas, rising up from the desert suddenly and inexplicably. It's smaller than Vegas, but just as jarring if you aren't expecting it.

That day, the sky was dusty blue and ragged clouds blew lazily across, north to south. The MWF building was on Parker Street, in the shadow of an overpass. It was a factory of some type at one time. It was two stories, had big metal rolltop doors, and big windows in the front. Inside, a long hall led out to the factory floor, which had been converted into a wrestling arena. A ring sat in the middle of the room, with metal gates blocking off the crowd seating—"seating" being just a bunch of metal folding chairs. An entrance ramp led to the backstage area. Locker rooms, toilets, some more offices.

"You must be Mr. DeNacco," someone said behind us.

We turned. The guy was short, scrawny, and balding, with big black glasses. "I'm Harold Kuntmyer. Mr. Watkins' booker."

Harold was the guy who ran the day-to-day operations of the company while Bill Watkins pissed his money away at craps and blackjack. He'd been active in the wrestling scene since the forties. He knew the business like the back of his hand, which pleased Tony. He had someone to take care of the heavy lifting.

We all went over to this diner across the highway and talked turkey awhile. Tony figured that after expenses (paying the wrestlers and shit) he could make about three Gs off the MWF. Half of that had to go to the big boss. It wasn't great, but it was money, and that's what the mob's all about. Better yet, it was clean money.

That was a Tuesday. The Saturday show was gonna be taped on Thursday. Me and Tony left Harold in charge of everything and returned to L.A. Thursday morning, Tony picked me up and we went back to Barstow. We met the wrestlers (all thirty of them) and watched from the sidelines as people started packing in. Attendance that night was two hundred. Not great, but whatever.

I'm not gonna go into details, but the night went good. The crowd loved it. The guys were good. The main event, pitting our biggest face (good guy) against our biggest heel (bad guy) was a real treat. Lotta blood. When the heel won and proceeded to work the crowd, shit went wild—people were throwing soda cans and popcorn boxes and everything.

"Who writes this shit?" I asked Harold.

"I do," he said. "For the most part. If a wrestler's big enough, he gets creative control. Sometimes that's a good thing. Sometimes it isn't."

Boy was he right.

Like I said earlier, that was in September 1973. In November, I got busted roughing a union worker up and got three years. But in those two months, I was in Barstow every week, sort of...rediscovering my love for wrestling. Uncle Tony stopping going after the second week and used me as his eyes and ears. I passed messages on to Harold, and he got them done. It was a fucking dream. I mean, it was lucky. We inherited this great promotion and a great right hand man. Shit rarely happens that easily.

Anyway, back to prison. I did my three years, didn't talk, didn't bother anyone, and got out a little early, in July instead of October. The first place I went was Uncle Tony's.

"I don't want you out there anymore," he said, hugging me. "I want you doing something else."

That "something else" wound up being the MWF full-time. He wanted me to be the jack-of-all-trades type—to head up security, book talent, come up with storyline angles. Whatever needed doing. I wouldn't be making big money, but I was okay with that. Uncle Tony bought me a car and got me an apartment in Barstow, and that was that. I was pretty much on my own.

For the first year or so, I stuck close to Harold, learning everything I could from the guy. How to do this, how to do that. We came up with a couple angles that went big, even got us in *Pro Wrestling Illustrated*, the biggest wrestling mag in the country. We did brisk business. Not too much more than when we started, yeah, but we were getting by fine.

Uncle Tony came by every once in a while to make sure things were going good, and they were. In June 1977, the NWA champ (who toured all the different promotions, giving the local heroes a shot at the gold) dropped the belt to our main guy ("Punishing" Paul Perry).Suddenly the wrestling community knew who we were—and people who didn't usually give a shit about it started coming by because, hey, they won the belt. We got a second TV timeslot in 1979. Friday Night Wrestling was carried all over the Mojave and into San Fran.

That summer, we toured a little. After getting permission from the NWA and the regional promoters, we did a show in L.A. in June, and another in Vegas in August. The first brought in 10,000 fans, the second 11,000. We were making more money than ever, and Uncle Tony started taking a more active interest. By the end of 1979, he was devoting more time to the MWF than the L.A. Family.

Then Vince McMahon took the WWF national.

Remember when I said earlier that wrestling worked on a territorial system? Well, there's a reason I said "back then." In 1980, Vince McMahon, a promoter in the Northeast, started buying out other promotions and their assets (including TV time). He envisioned a huge money-making corporation spanning the country. I can't say I blame the guy, it was ambitious, but that's not how wrestling worked. He pissed a lot of people off with that.

Uncle Tony was one of them.

In March, McMahon made Tony a lowball offer to buy the MWF and turn it into a "real" promotion. Tony told him to go to hell and hung up. He was so offended that he said we should start buying other promotions and go nationwide too. Sort of a war. Anyone who knows anything about wrestling knows what happened to WCW when they went up against WWF. They made good ratings, but after a while they lost steam, and one day, old Vinnie McMahon came calling with a briefcase full of cash. I was for the idea. Let's do it, I said. Tony kinda backed down once he did the math. He did buy a couple TV timeslots from failing promotions out east. He also gave me permission to start luring McMahon's talent away.

"Money's no problem on that front," he said, "because fuck that guy."

I offered top dollar to WWF guys, and most of them took it. Some of these meatheads were nationally famous by then, and people wanted to see them. We bought a few timeslots from other companies across the country, ticking off the NWA in the process. In 1981, they excluded us from hosting the NWA champion, so we scratched all the championship belts to shit, sent them to NWA headquarters, and replaced them with our own belts. In retaliation, the NWA kicked us out.

I know I've been rambling. Here's the good part:

In 1983, at a WWF event in Fresno, I got backstage and managed to talk to a few of their guys. None of them seemed interested in my offer except for a big, towering hunk of meat named Krusher Kompanski. Real name Hiram Kompanski, he debuted with the WWF in '81 after wrestling under a variety of names in the South and Midwest. On TV he was a giant, but in person he was even bigger: 6'5, 300 pounds (all muscle), and arms like fucking tree trunks. Standing next to him, I felt like a kid. He wore this black leotard and a leather mask. When he cut promos, he didn't talk, just grunted and made crushing gestures with his hands. *"Crush! Crush!"* he'd yell.

Of course that was all an act. He wasn't the smartest guy, but he was a lot smarter than some of the goons Tony had working for him back in L.A. He said he wasn't happy in the WWF because he couldn't develop his own character. They told him to be the big, dumb wildman or get the fuck out. Because he was popular, and his contract was (serendipitously) about to expire, I told him I'd give him more money than Vince McMahon and let him develop his own character.

We shook.

Krusher Kompanski debuted in the MWF on October 3, 1983, running to the ring to save our biggest heel (Slim Jim Robinson) from a beatdown by the good guys. I was at the announcers' table that night because I wanted to see him in action, and I'm glad I was. Kompanski was a beast. Despite his massive size, he ran quickly and silently to the ring, slid under the bottom rope, and started kicking tail. The fans recognized him right away, and started cheering their asses off. Backstage after the show, I shook his hand and said, "You're fucking great. Oh, man, that was good."

He smiled. "Thanks. I think so too."

By December, Krusher Kompanski was our main guy. In the MWF, he wasn't a big, dumb wildman—he was a psychopathic juggernaut who just liked hurting people. Our TV timeslots around the country blew up; everyone wanted to see what the wildman would do next. Would he hit a ref? Maybe. Would he snatch an announcer up and clobber him over the head? Who knows? By the beginning of 1984, me and Uncle Tony were beginning to think we'd have enough capital to go up against the WWF by 1985, maybe 1986 at the latest.

Two things stopped us.

One: Carmine Guggio, boss of the family, started demanding bigger cuts from our profit. "You guys are on TV every week," he said. "I go to look for news, I come across your guys playing tiddly-winks on Channel 3. You're making more money, so you give me more money. It's only fair."

Two: Krusher Kompanski himself. We were building our brand around the guy, and he knew it. The sneaky son of a bitch knew he was our star, and he started milking it. He wanted more money, he wanted more control, he wanted to choose his matches. He was a fucking primadonna. Poor old Harold, sixty-two and sickly, nearly lost his mind dealing with that asshole. Kompanski'd fucking whine like a little bitch. "I don't liiiiiike that." "I don't waaaaana lose to him." Finally, Harold retired. He was dead in a year anyway, but I think he woulda stayed until the bitter end if it wasn't for that fat piece of shit.

Tony didn't like Kompanski, but he knew which side his bread was buttered on, so he gave in where he could. From October 1983 to March 1984, Kompanski didn't lose a single match. Looking back in hindsight, I guess it was a good angle. You know, crazy man just knocking out the competition. The WCW did it with Goldberg in the late nineties. That wasn't our plan, though. We were gonna have him get beat in mid-'84 by the main face (Bob Davis), but Kompanski wouldn't have it.

Things came to a head in April. Kompanski already lost to Davis the month before and he was scheduled for another loss. He bitched and moaned in my ear for three weeks. Then all the other wrestlers were bitching at me because he was so hard to work with. It was a fucking nightmare.

Anyway, on April 10, Krusher Kompanski went up against Gene Terry, a short, skinny little kid we were working as the underdog. Kompanski was going to be his first win.

The problem? When the match started, Kompanski wouldn't sell anything the kid did. That means, when Terry threw a punch (not connecting, because wrestling's fake, remember?), Kompanski just stood there, lookin at him. The kid was supposed to get Kompanski up on his shoulders and bring him down on the ring (collapsing it in the process), but when he tried, Kompanski just shoved him aside like he was flea.

"That's not in the fucking script," I said. Me and Uncle Tony were in the back, watching on a TV monitor. Finally, Kompanski snatched the kid up by his throat and gave him a real slam to the mat. You could see it on the kid's face—it hurt. Kompanski put his boot on the kid's chest, and the ref had no choice but to count one-two-three.

"That Polack motherfucker!" I tore off the headphones and stood up.

Tony put a hand on my arm. "Cool it, will you?"

"He just fucked up the match! On purpose!"

Tony nodded. "That's okay. He'll get his."
I knew instantly what he was talking about.

Remember how I said the NWA was like the mob? Well, one of the common practices throughout the wrestling world was to have veteran guys sort of police the locker rooms. If anyone did anything wrong (like purposely flub a match because they were a big whiny bitch), the vets would take care of it in the ring. They'd really hurt the other guy. As in: "This shit isn't fake, that guy just really got his nose broken."

Really.

Krusher Kompanski was going to get his. April 15.

Me and Tony had fun planning it. We'd have Kompanski go up against Bob Davis. Bob would kick Kompanski in the nuts, then whip out a blackjack and work his head over. The ref would ring for a disqualification, but who cared? After security came to fetch Kompanski's fat ass, they'd take him out in the parking lot and beat even more shit out him. It was a fitting punishment. There were gonna be at least three hundred people in the arena, and hundreds more watching at home. Humble his ass, you know?

The Davis/Kompanski match was the main event of the evening. I was worried about Kompanski getting the upper hand, so I had security and the other wrestlers on alert, just in case. If something went wrong, they'd all go out to the ring.

Anyway, it was late when the match started, maybe nine. The match before Kompanski's ran over because the guy who was supposed to win broke his ankle jumping off the turnbuckle—and he and his opponent had to come up with another, unscripted end on the fly. That was teamwork. Something Kompanski didn't know anything about.

Davis and Kompanski stuck to the script for the first five minutes. Then, when Davis had Kompanski in the corner, he let fly and nailed the sorry dick-breath right in the sack.

Believe it or not, Kompanski didn't cry out, he didn't double over, and he didn't fall down. He just stood up taller, as if to say, *Oh, that's how it's gonna be?*

Sure enough, he grabbed Bob Davis up by the throat and started squeezing. The ref, in the loop, tried to break it up, but Kompanski shoved him away.

The ref signaled, and the bell rang: Disqualified.

Not that it mattered. Bob Davis was turning blue. Then, with a taunting flourish, Kompanski drove his fist into Davis's stomach once, twice, three times.

"Goddamn it!" I growled. Tony didn't say anything.

Kompanski lifted Bob above his head and threw him out of the ring. He came down on the announcers' table (which didn't break because it hadn't been cut beforehand), and slid off.

I ripped off the headphones and stormed out of the control booth. The locker rooms were just down the hall. The guys were sitting around, talking, smoking, and laughing. When they saw me, red-faced and hissing, they perked up.

"Ring! Now!"

They all nodded, said "Yes, boss," and whatever, and started toward the ring.

Back in the control booth, I sat down, snatched up my headphones, and put them back on. On the screen, Kompanski was ripping the ring apart. The top rope hung limply from the turnbuckle, which was slanted like an ancient tombstone in an even more ancient cemetery. "What the fuck is he doing?"

"He's going fucking nuts," Tony said.

The first wrestlers hit the ring, sliding under the bottom rope. Kompanski's back was turned. The first hit him hard, but then Kompanski turned around and caught him by the neck. Every two seconds, someone else hit the ring. There were like twenty guys. It was crazy.

Even crazier, Kompanski was winning.

Punch, punch, headlock. Bodies were dropping and flying over the top rope left and right. One of my guys had a steel pipe (a real steel pipe, not that foam crap), and he hit Kompanski square in the face with it. The fucker didn't even notice; he just grabbed the guy and flung him into the turnbuckle, knocking another wrestler down in the process.

Another guy hit Kompanski with a pair of brass knuckles, but he wound up with a broken back from hitting the gate separating the ring from the fans dead-on—so a lot of good *that* did him.

By then, blood was pouring off Kompasnki in rivulets. He choke-slammed one guy, elbowed another behind him in the face, then snatched a baseball bat from a third and hit him so hard, it ended his career right there.

"Security!" I yelled.

Tony was transfixed. "Jesus Christ."

Before you could say "Kill that son of a bitch," the ring area was flooded with guys in yellow shirts. They had batons and Tasers.

They hit the ring as one, but Kompanski was ready. He snatched the first one up, twisted his arm behind his back until he screamed, and then threw him into the rest. They swarmed him like ants on a dead body, but he threw them off like they were nothing. I know like hell I saw him get tazed at least a dozen times, but it didn't faze him. I couldn't believe it.

Of course, the fans were going crazy. It was the best damn thing they ever seen.

On the screen, Kompanski ripped out one of the turnbuckle pikes and swung it at the security guards, hitting one in the head and nearly killing him. They came forward again, but with one swing, Kompanski took them all out. I swear to God, he musta took on fifty guys that night.

But that wasn't the end.

He climbed over the top rope and started back up the entrance ramp.

With a dropping heart, I knew where he was going.

"That crazy son of a bitch," Tony muttered. "What's he doing now?"

"He's coming for us!" I said, standing up.

Tony opened his mouth to argue, but before he could, a loud crash filled the hall. "Jimmy! Tony!" Krusher Kompanski screamed.

Tony's eyes went wide and he struggled to his feet. "Lock the door," he said.

I sprang forward and turned the thumb lock. The door was a piece of shit. It wouldn't hold up long against Krusher Kompanski.

"You made a big mistake tonight!" Kompanski screamed. More crashing. He was tearing down the house as he came.

I reached into my jacket and pulled out the big Colt Python I kept in a shoulder ring. Tony's eyes widened. "What are you doing?"

"I'm gonna kill this motherfucker," I said. To my ears, I sounded more scared than anything else.

Tony shook his head.

Kompanski was at the door. One punch, and the thing flew off the hinges, skidding halfway across the room before crashing to the floor. I turned, startled, and the monster himself filled the threshold—big, huffing, and covered in blood. He looked like a bull—a bull that fucking ate people whole and spat out their skeletons.

"Come here, Jimmy!"

I raised the gun. "You asked for it!"

He started toward me, and I fired, the sound of the blast like a cannon in the confined space. Kompanski jerked, but he didn't stop. Hell, he didn't even slow.

"I'm going to kill you!" he screamed.

Tony was behind me now, cowering. I fired again, and again. Kompanski jerked as both bullets hit him in the chest.

I put one his stomach.

That one slowed him. Blood was gushing now. He pushed himself on, like a man trudging through three feet of snow.

I aimed directly at Kompanski's head and fired.

Like a massive Cali redwood, Kompanski swayed, toppled, and crashed to the floor.

He was dead.

With all the controversy surrounding the death of Krusher Kompanski, Tony decided to sell the MWF.

But not to Vince McMahon.

Owing to the destruction and the thirty-five plus assaults (some of them were technically classified as attempted murder), the shooting was declared to have been done in self-defense and I was cleared of any wrongdoing. A famous doctor in L.A. claimed that Kompanski most likely lapsed into a sort of rage-fueled blackout, rendering him unable to control himself and granting him superhuman strength. I don't know if that's what happened or not, and I really don't care. That motherfucker deserved it either way.

Hall of Fame my ass.

The Calumet

by Amanda Marbais

Liz was parked in an industrial corridor of Gary watching stray dogs dig in the dirt of an abandoned lot. The paper factory chugged a cloud of sulfides enveloping the houses in the scent of wet wool and cabbage. Liz smoked out of her cracked window despite frozen-white fingers and blue nail beds, an idiot for freezing, waiting, and for being conspicuous. She texted her boyfriend—*Get up douche, or we're done.* She honked. No Rich. She was beginning to wonder if their static was becoming radio silence.

She reached for another cigarette and felt around in her half-zipped duffle bag. There was the reassurance of the thick envelope of cash from the sale of her Toyota. Her mom had padded that payout for sure, because she was a better person than Liz. All her cash in the world, and it was starting to make her paranoid. She slammed on the horn again. A dog barked. Rich's battered front door didn't open.

Of course, Rich was hung over from the Low Down last night and gun-shy about what they had decided to do to Janet. Honestly, Liz was scared too. But, they needed to move on this or spend another year in Gary.

She pressed the horn for a full three seconds. Nothing. A cruiser turned the corner, creeping past the factory gate. There were always police in this neighborhood and honking only brought them closer, the equivalent of shark-chum. They had to investigate everything. Two forms of job security in this town: cops, and crime scene cleanup. The cop passed Liz and looked in the car, a dude with a big mustache and mutton chops creeping over his cheeks like an illness. She sent Rich the text, *Walk, asshole*, and hit the gas before Serpico could turn around.

Rich had been so excited about their plan to cheat Janet, it surprised Liz he was screwing it up. A walking disaster, Janet would sit at the dingy Low Down and openly admit her toddler slept unsupervised a block away. Like every stripper, she was ridiculously skinny, bony limbs like a praying mantis. Whenever she did bumps without going to the bathroom, Ronnie, the owner, would tell her, "No drama." Despite having slept with Janet, Ronnie gave her no slack either. A lot of people in Gary wished the worst on Janet.

"Janet, I wish half your bullshit was true," Rich had said after his fifth shot of Red Stag. He and Janet had gone to high school together. Of course, that's not why he believed her. Rich was always hopeful a scam would pay out. He sat forward on the red vinyl bench listening, his eyelids licking back over ghost-like orbs. He worked his mouth, wanting Janet's alleged stash to be real with the same anxiety he displayed at any difficult situation—anxiety floating above him like a Tesla sphere.

It amazed Liz that Janet had been her first friend since leaving New York, and they once spent every night at the Low Down getting wasted. It was the kind of bar where a country band performed behind a cage of chicken wire. The walls were decorated with beer signs, and on weekdays, Credence blared like it was 1975. Occasionally there was an Eminem track. Liz wasn't proud of using Janet to unload as she verbalized the worst of her past. Janet was the kind of girl who took it and was too insecure to say no.

In turn, Janet drilled out tales about her movie "star" granddad, Dick Jarmen, who was an extra on *Bonanza* for three seasons, gave up and returned home to collect

Medicaid. She bullshitted with anyone in earshot. People grew weary of it and moved tables. Ronnie pretended he didn't know her. But, everyone around here had a brush-with-fame story.

Last night, Rich and his friend Derek listened to Janet's bullshit about a mountain of meth worth seventy-five thousand, enough to get anyone out of Gary. Derek was one of those friends Liz hung out with, the one friend left over from Rich's "less than aboveboard" days. Together, Rich and Derek had tried so many marginal activities—a little bit of insurance fraud, a car scam he didn't really explain, and skimming credit cards at Gas Depot.

Lately, Derek worked at one of the clean-up companies, Clean City!, and had done a meth job until 6am. A fucking bear trap had been hidden under some blankets. A crew member walked right into it. "Sliced to the ankle bone," Derek had said. They got off early. He'd been resting his head on the back of the booth, motionless for a half-hour like the taxidermied elk above him. But when Janet said three pounds, Derek sat up as if someone were already throwing free money through the bar. "We could sell it for you," he said.

"I dunno. It's going to be shit anyway," said Rich. But he was already getting that vulnerable-yet-crazy look where money was concerned. When he and Derek talked money, they grew desperate, words gathering in a power-source with the potential to light a city, creating their own grid. They could pull it from nowhere.

"It's good stuff," said Janet.

"Why would a guy with that much product hang out with you, anyway?" said Rich.

Janet was leaned back so that her hair was tinged blue by the flickering neon Milwaukee's Best sign inches above her. "He just likes what I give him, man," she said.

"Janet, you pick the worst guys. You can't see shit in the opposite sex. I told you that in high school," said Rich.

"I'm not really into him. I'm waiting around to take his shit, because he hit my kid and all."

"Rich, none of this is true," said Liz.

"I've known Janet a long time," said Rich. "She doesn't lie when it counts."

"That's exactly when she lies," said Liz.

Liz's real hate for Janet could be summed up in one incident. Last summer, Janet left her three-year-old, Destiny, in a car for five hours, windows rolled up, ninety-degree heat. The kid's lips were a dry, puckered crater in her face. And even in the hospital, she wouldn't drink for hours. They hooked an IV to the kid, who was one giant blister in the white hospital sheets.

"I'm no skank, like you, Liz," said Janet. "I didn't have no three-way with these dudes. That's why I can't be friends with a person like you. Sorry."

Liz rolled her eyes. "Janet. Shut up."

Janet, eyes still on Liz, opened her purse slightly and aimed it toward the table revealing a Ziploc of meth—800 labs shut down, and the stuff still floated around in the coffee shops, the rest stops of Gary.

Rich had barely let his eyes flit down, but he was looking. "See babe? I told you she didn't lie about important stuff."

"I just can't find anyone to buy it," said Janet.

"I know people," said Derek before he started laughing, a deep rumble like the sound of a freight truck passing. But that's when Ronnie had turned up the music and gave them the get-the-fuck-out look. Rich and Derek had grown jumpy.

Talking a mile a minute, they made an arrangement for the consignment situation—a small amount of cash up front, courtesy of Liz, and a quarter of the proceeds down the line. They'd meet at Victor's Tap the next night, and make a trade. They were gulping the last of their beers when Ronnie kicked them out.

Issue Eighteen

By the time she hit the highway towards Victor's Tap, Liz was pissed as hell at Rich for sleeping away his hangover. She would have to stall Janet while Rich dragged his ass out of bed. So much for them coordinating shit. She reached over to the passenger's seat and opened her duffle again to recheck it. She had clothes, shampoo, weed, a toothbrush, and *Fight Club*, the last book she'd read for college, back when she was still an Environmental Studies major, floating to class, buffeted safely on a river of students. She ran out of money, and she didn't want a hundred grand in debt. Something more immediate was needed. Before driving to Rich's, she'd spent the morning packing at her one-room rental while her landlady downstairs, a single woman named Ms. Turley, cranked a *Lifetime* TV movie, feeding two Retrievers Cheetos and shouting commands.

Rich had said, "Once we get the money, let's crash at your mom's in Chicago." But, when they got to Chicago, she wouldn't be stopping home. She'd see her mother when things improved. To witness the worry Rich would inspire in her mother would be too much.

Liz felt burned out from the last year. Whatever she had done, she didn't want to get caught or fucked over. She pulled her grandma's hand-me-down Buick into a Citgo and parked under the glow of an orange light. Everything from the stacked tires to the white smoke pluming from the smokestacks drove her nuts. She put her head on the steering wheel, in dread over her shit decisions.

When she lifted her head, a guy pumping gas was staring. His kid in the backseat looked up from his iPad and stared too. Hands fluttering, she opened the envelope, fifteen thousand deep—a fat haul. She suspected the extra money her mom threw in was from the sale of Grandma's house. She wondered again how her mother could be so much better than her.

Some dude walked past on his way to the highway and turned toward the car. "Keep walking," said Liz. She would have run him over for half this money. He kept walking.

What to do with the money? Rich hadn't been right since he lost his dad. Rich and his dad had been on a hundred hunting trips, Indiana's pastime. Liz thought the 12-gauge in the face was intentional. She'd never tell Rich that, since he found his dad still harnessed to the tree stand. In a way she wasn't good for Rich, since she couldn't reach in and find any strength, any sympathy. If he mentioned the word Dad, she was immediately back in her own home.

She pulled two thousand—a little insurance—from the envelope, rolled it in a pair of underwear, and wedged it in the metal supports under the seat. Rich complained of her glibness and insincerity over his dad's death once he began a cocktail of Olanzapine and Depakote, which gave him a brief calm. She decided to go back to Chicago. But when she was leaving, he freaked out. Folded like a paper-doll in their kitchen, split his lip from the fall. She held his face between her hands, watched his chest rise and fall, blue eyes focusing and receding. He went from sadistic and strong to being reminiscent of a tagged deer, his sharp features and pale brown hair, blood trickling over one blank eye. She took care of him for days, kept him from sleeping in his car when paranoia drove him to find a safe space.

For someone living in a city where the drinking water was suspect and the air quality was a breath of cancer, he was incredibly optimistic. He was just waiting for this Janet thing, or something like it. Of course it was one last trip "below board," as he put it. He'd gone off the meds a month before. Running and lifting weights had become his answer for everything. Even though he was drunk last night, he'd still jogged three miles, had come home shouting about meth labs and dead animals in the abandoned lot.

When she followed him to Gary, when they'd given up on New York, she discovered this town *was* Rich. Park waters a beautiful polluted green and failed manufacturing. Liz gripped the wheel and leaned hard on the gas. She was greeted with fifty billboards on the highway:

Had an accident? Suffering from Black Lung, Cancer, Emphysema? Free Complete Pulmonary Evaluation. Don't give up. Plinski and Danforth can help!

Night Angels Gentleman's Club.

Whispers. Discount Furs. Impress her!

Yep. Fast money.

Rich still hadn't texted when Liz pulled into Victor's Steak and Tap, the last strip club before the Illinois state line. It was a favorite not just with truckers, but with people not wanting to pay Chicago's strip club prices. It was a strange crowd. It had a few patrons who looked burned out and ready to hide.

She parked behind the building, hiding her car from the road. She lit a cigarette, struggled with her prescription. She needed people with their shit together. She craved it. But she also wanted people who were real, and that was sort of the rub, why she moved someplace rural. Her mom's family and friends were fake. Brooklyn had been full of fakes. Now she was way the hell and gone from where she thought she would be. She tipped her head back, swallowed, put the envelope in her purse.

Inside, she scanned Victor's. Janet was nowhere. Liz sat down at the bar, ordered a whiskey and waited for the Xanax to kick in.

This was one of those dive places to strip. She had always done better, made a grand a night. Don't talk to her about daddy issues or hearts of gold. That was the mythology of stripping. And she had no problem going back if needed.

But dancing at this place would be like working at Denny's if you were a good waitress. Depressing. She downed her whiskey and ordered another. A dude with longish black hair who looked out of place was giving her the eye. He looked like Joaquin Phoenix.

Her phone buzzed. Rich. *Where the fuck are you?*

Victor's. Answer your texts next time! No response. She laid down a veiled 'fuck you.' *Get a ride with Derek!*

Derek managed to be less reliable than Rich. If Rich was Gary, Derek was Gary's dirty cousin. His ass was supposed to be at Victor's too. Of course, he was nowhere to be found. Liz had texted him too. Surprise. No response.

Joaquin's double was giving her a gross look, but she was bored, so she didn't stop him from taking the seat beside her. "Hey, I'm Cary."

He smiled at her and continued, "You wouldn't believe it. They were shooting a movie down at the river. Some cop show," he said. He was drunk but still seemed a little dangerous.

"No they weren't," said Liz. She shot her whiskey to make it more tolerable to talk to him.

"Is that hard to believe? I guess beautiful girls have a hard time believing second-hand stories."

"It's a little early to flirt like your life depended on it."

"Don't flatter yourself. Did you ever see *Silence of the Lambs*?" said Cary.

"Everyone has seen *The Silence of the Lambs*." She stressed the word *The*. He didn't notice.

"You know how that guy just fools girls into getting into his van?"

"That movie is so disturbing."

"But, you know what I'm talking about?"

"I've seen the movie. It's on cable all the time, dipshit."

"Well, you know how he just gets them to climb in the back of the truck, and then like pushes that heavy piece of furniture into them? Then he gets them to his house. But after he kills them, he weights them in the river. "

Liz hoped he wasn't the kind of drunk to spool out unconscious thoughts. "It wasn't my favorite movie." She slowly wiped her mouth and raised her hand for another drink.

"Doesn't have to be. I'm just saying, that down there by the river, they had kind of one of those dead-body-in-the-reeds-thing happening. And, that's what they were filming."

"Really?" She tried to convey she wasn't interested. She stopped mid-sip, when the bartender gave her the "too-fast" eye. Everyone feels they need to parent an attractive woman. But they can fuck off.

"Yeah. It's hidden back on the Calumet. I guess they're going to make money in some poor town where they don't have to pay much to use the land. Movies are kind of a big business, what with all the franchises."

Liz turned to look at him like he wasn't for real.

"It's all the Marvel Comic adaptations," said Cary.

Something in this dude reminded her of her brother. He and her mom were huge film nerds. The three of them went to The Music Box weekly. She relaxed a little. "You seem like a freak for movies." *And also an idiot*, she thought.

"Me and my mom used to go a lot. When I lived in the city," said Cary.

They swapped stories about Chicago. Liz had forgotten Janet, and was drunk by the time Derek arrived and gave her a shitty look. "Bitch," he mouthed from the door. He walked up to Cary, picked up the dude's whiskey and downed it. "Fuck off," he said.

Cary laughed.

"Derek," said Liz. She put a hand over her drink and smiled up at him.

Derek said nothing, but nodded toward the back of the bar, where Janet sat alone in a booth, looking freaked out.

"You fucked up, Liz," said Derek.

Liz realized she had been talking to this dope, Cary, long enough to miss Janet's arrival. Fuck. Liz threw down a twenty. "Nice talking to you."

Rich was standing at the door. He had spotted her and looked super-pissed she was talking to some dude. Rich was sensitive, but everyone was, so Liz couldn't fault him. It was hard to tell when someone was really going to leave. Once he became jealous over a bartender hitting on her, and he called her nothing but "slut" for a month. She'd matched him with "pussy" for that same month, aware of the irony. To her, it wasn't a bad thing. Fuck him if he took it negatively. She wanted to explain the irony to him, but didn't have the energy.

When they walked to the table, Liz tried to pry her mind out of the film talk—specifically *The 400 Blows*, which she had studied in film class. Cary was going on about it. Some dude in Indiana knew about French New Wave. Amazing. She couldn't get her head back on their task and Rich looked like an alien, sad and pathetic, just staring at her.

He took her arm. "I called you," he said.

Liz pulled her arm away.

"I didn't see you guys. I thought you pussed out," said Janet. She smoked her cigarette incredibly fast. She was so high, the words spilled out in an explanation of what she'd done since they saw her.

"Let's go outside," said Derek.

"Wait a sec. Are we leaving?" said Liz.

"I ain't doing shit here," said Derek.

Rich's fingers pressed into her upper arm, and he smelled of cigarettes and booze. The thrash metal made it hard to hear, so she leaned closer. "Let's get this done," he said. It sounded meaningful, but he was looking at Derek.

There were those times in Liz's life when a realization began to surface, but retreated again without warning—some small fish swimming to the top of her consciousness. Who knew what it meant? But, she stood there and blinked.

"Hold on. I have to piss," she said. She wrenched her arm away, and Rich looked at the floor. "That's what I thought," she said. Whatever optimism he exuded last night was gone, and his expression had become one of terror.

Liz ran to the bathroom, feeling nauseated and breathing heavily. She reached into her purse, pulled out the envelope and fumbled with it. She stopped. She took a deep breath and wished she were already in Chicago. She could just walk out and tell Rich to fuck off, drive to see her mom, who would listen without judgment. She stared at her reflection in the mirror, her pale skin feathered with lines. She pulled two grand from her thick stack. She would give them the two grand, say she wouldn't have the rest until Monday. She'd say her mom still had it. It was safe.

Someone was knocking. "Fucking wait a second," she said. She reached into the paper towel dispenser, slid the large stack—eleven thousand minus the two—as far up as she could get it. She scraped her hand on the lip of the dispenser trying to do it.

"Hurry the fuck up," a woman yelled through the door.

She thrust her hand under the sink tap. She could easily get this when she came back for her car. If something worse happened, some stripper would find it when washing the stink off. More power to that bitch. This place was an inglorious, industrialized strip-tank. Hopefully, she would realize she could do better.

She cleaned away the makeup smudges in the mirror and walked out.

Rich was waiting. "What the fuck? Are you trying to make me crazy?"

"Nothing," said Liz.

"Don't ruin this," said Rich.

After all that, Rich and Derek "had to talk to the owner" and made Liz and Janet wait outside not speaking, Janet slowly sipping her flask and staring at the highway. "You're an awful bitch," said Liz.

Janet took a drink from her flask and didn't turn around. Whatever camaraderie there was between the dudes inside, it was totally gone between Janet and Liz. Shivering, Liz watched the highway too.

Derek and Rich came out. Rich told Janet. "We'll follow."

"Another location?" said Janet.

"I said we ain't talking here," said Rich.

They followed Janet's Chevy past Denny's, the Citgo, out of Gary, and south on the highway. Liz thought of Cary, her family, and school. She watched Rich drink bourbon from a Coke bottle, smoke a cigarette. Liz rubbed her arm absently where he'd grabbed her. The soreness was small, a bloom that promised to open larger.

When his depression would hit, Rich could be nearly immobilized. Last time he hit bottom, he didn't leave the apartment in Bushwick for days and Liz was surprised he didn't off himself. But once he could crawl his way out of the mud, he came up swinging. She'd mistakenly thought he was brooding, only to find out he was mentally ill. Then the Olanzapine.

Rich turned around, eyes narrow, a perfectly rigid face, Plasticine. He had explained this plan like she were a child as they ate Thai food at this dive near her crappy rental. Janet had come by the stuff by screwing a dealer.

"You think it's stolen?" said Liz.

"I know it is. Now she's going to steal it from that jackass Tom."

"Not surprising."

"Nobody gives a shit about her," he said.

"Yeah."

"It's not like she's a good person anyway. She's a cock-sucking thief," he said.

Calling Janet a cocksucker was, at best, obvious. Liz hated it when Rich said stupid things. But, it also inspired pathos, which she couldn't resist.

"It'll be easy. I promise," he said.

Liz didn't mind double-crossing Janet either. She felt like everyone had a part to play, and Janet was playing the victim this time. It became clear they were going to make Janet the dog in this. Liz had been the dog before, so it was only fair she come out on top this time.

Derek was driving like a maniac past the wind farms. He grumbled that Janet was speeding up. "She's trying to get away," he said.

"Why the fuck would she do that?" said Rich.

"Because she doesn't have dick. She smoked it all," said Derek.

"I'll beat the shit out of her if that's the case."

"You're always talking big," said Liz. She lit a cigarette. "If she smoked it that fast, she'd be dead."

"Fuck you, Liz." Derek looked at Rich nervously, to see if he crossed a line. But, Rich didn't care. Apparently, he wanted to be defended. He cleared his throat and threw his cigarette out the passenger window.

There were a couple weeks, when they all first met, when Liz had been intermittently sleeping with both of them. In Derek's more contemplative moods, he rambled about his days as a Marine. It nearly always degenerated into a rhetorical discussion of violence, in which Derek stared off in the distance. It felt stagey. Liz distrusted that he was ever sad about killing people. She doubted he really knew the difference between the real and the unreal. He was pissed when she ended it. But, how could she deal with his profound ambivalence?

She took out her phone and checked her messages, texted a friend from Chicago, and slipped the phone into her coat, watching the towering poles, the airplane propellers spinning slowly in lazy discontinuity. Rich gave her a half-smile with a crooked attempt at levity, reached back, and smacked her leg.

"C'mon. It's easy," he said.

"It's not," said Liz.

"She kind of deserves it." He raised an eyebrow and made a face.

"That may be true," said Liz. "We all kind of deserve shitty things."

Last fall she'd had a particularly rough time with Rich. It was partly her fault. She had her head in the clouds, constantly oscillating between thinking too largely, and letting herself drop back to reality, knowing all the while, you had to work with your own assets. She stopped stripping for a while. She cried a lot.

He was always having those crazy stars in his eyes. Rich could fool people, because he could be fooled himself. He was always lured by money. And, he wanted all of it. He could be greedy. Last time he thought he had a fast deal turning over those cars with Derek, he'd really gotten in shape. Talked only of money. He kept his body perfect, ran each morning, coming home in his sweats, flushed. He looked good. He'd cook deer meat in the slow cooker, his mom's recipe. Predictably, he talked about his parents then.

It was at that moment she couldn't stand him. She felt mismatched, like his bullshit was hers. But, she did want to protect them both. With the fifty thousand, they were going to get an apartment in Roger's Park, better jobs, a better shrink. Liz would go back to school, and if they parted ways, they'd both be better off. She hadn't told him yet.

On a dirt road, they paralleled the river, past poplars and oaks heavy with snow, half-shattered sheets of river ice where the water sometimes bubbled through the fissures like oil. They were headed into the woods. No one driving by would notice them, but you could still catch sight of the highway over the rise. There was one burned-out building, but nothing else. Shit. It was poor here. But beautiful. New York had its interesting neighborhoods, museums, but let's face it, she spent most of her time in her hovel in Bushwick. New York was for the rich.

The low-hanging branches spanned the road, as if heavy with child, and reached backward toward the rushing water. But the area was deserted, and she thought about Victor's and the Low Down and Ms. Turley. If you wanted decline, but beauty, this was the film location.

They pulled into an empty campsite and parked near a pit of charred wood. They got out of Derek's car and he walked around to the trunk, where he pulled out some Budweisers and set the six-pack on a log. "Here they are," he said. As if the beer had been missing.

Liz watched the Calumet rush by, destined for its putrescent state by the lake. People still fished and swam in Lake Michigan where the Calumet rushed in, filled with industrial runoff and pollution. She marveled at the swift current, free of large debris, brownish-gray, fast and deep.

Derek and Rich exchanged looks and were shotgunning their beers, too busy drinking to speak. Rich was entering one of those bipolar descents where it looked like he didn't even know her, like he could see right through to the back of her skull. It chilled the fuck out of her.

Liz began to worry about everything now. "What if Janet doesn't have it on her?"

"She's got it," said Derek. "I seen it in her purse."

"Does she have both bags?" said Liz. "Because we need all three pounds."

"She does." Derek looked at Rich.

Janet got out of the car. "You got my fucking money," she said. "I'm done dicking around with this." She came toward them.

Liz opened her mouth to tell Janet it was a consignment deal; that was Liz's role—the mouthpiece. She was going to tell her there was only two grand, down from fifteen—sorry about your fucking luck. Then when the argument started, Rich and Derek would take over. No rough stuff. But, Janet and her drugs would part ways. Sometimes Liz hated herself. In those few seconds, Liz sensed she would come out with scars, collateral damage for involving herself with the wrong people, the wrong shit.

"Janet, this is how it's going to go down." Liz's voice grew large.

"Don't you fucking talk to me. I'm dealing with them."

Liz was ready to put Janet in her place, but a car turned off the highway and distracted her. Across the field, past an expanse of white, there was a growing bloom of whipping snow as an old Chevy sped down the dirt road. They were so far out in the middle of nothing. *Undercover cop*, thought Liz.

"Who the fuck is that?" said Janet.

The car gathered speed, spraying up snow and mud. The driver seemed too drunk to be the police. Liz's neck prickled, a snaking up, like cold water thrown over her bare back. She kept thinking *fuck*.

Fuck. Fuck.

Like it was the only word left in her mind. And she began regretting everything, even being alive.

She wondered if maybe it was what some people in this Bible Belt town called the Holy Spirit. But she didn't believe in that shit, and she hated herself for being reductive. She was feeling freaked out, and that's all. The car slammed to a stop.

Somehow she was not entirely surprised to see Cary. Something hadn't felt right about it. He was too smug. He wore steel-toed boots, had a gun visible beneath his open jacket.

"Hello, you pussies."

He pulled his gun out and so did Derek—something from the military, a high-grade weapon, probably illegal. They pointed them at Janet. Only Rich looked rabbity, frightened, like he might fly apart. Liz silently willed him to look at her. When Derek yelled something unintelligible, Rich pulled out a gun as well.

Someone shot Janet, who fell over lightly, like she'd just lost her balance, like she'd been walking along and slipped on the ice. She put her hands up to her cheek, smearing mud over her face, blood shooting from her ear and neck. It didn't last. She settled down softly, eyes open.

"Holy shit," said Liz. "Holy shit." She was the only one without a gun. But only one shot killed Janet, and it was from the psycho she'd met at the bar. Jesus, she should trust her instincts. She stood still, feeling like an idiot.

Rich looked freaked. "Oh baby. Oh baby," he said. He actually hopped around.

"C'mon. Do it," said Cary.

"Christ almighty. Fuckity-fuck," said Rich.

"Calm the fuck down," said Cary. "There's no splitting. And you pussies can't do the shit work."

Liz stood still in the cold, unable to stop considering how stupid Rich sounded for saying 'fuckity-fuck.' She didn't want this to be her last thought, but she couldn't help herself. *Fuckity-fuck. Fuckity-fuck.* He even stuttered.

"We have somewhere to be," said Cary. "And it's going to suck to bury these bodies in the dark. Ground's frozen enough."

"Wait," said Rich. Had he somehow had a change of heart? Even Liz knew they would shoot her no matter what.

Cary raised his gun, shot her in the leg. She could hear screams, but they were Rich's, as if he had been the one shot.

"Nope. Done deal," said Cary. "Like so many other things, lost in the river."

Again, Liz regretted that this blowhard's words would be the last she heard as she lay in the snow, thigh on fire and fighting the slip towards passing out.

"You fucking crazy asshole," said Rich.

"Too late," said Cary.

Derek stood above her not looking like himself. He aimed at her chest, as if he couldn't stand to mar her face. How stupid. It would feel like a force, a hard weight crushing her. Her death wasn't even her own, like a movie, however cliché that thought was—just another girl not reading the signs properly, partially to be blamed, no better or worse than anyone else. She came to the realization, she'd been bored for months, and now she wasn't. She began to regret.

Rich was shivering, holding his gun loosely as he slowly drew his skinny arms over his chest. He stared straight at her. He grew dimmer as she imagined some bitch getting the money before he did, his optimism finally meeting an end. Thank god. They'd never bury her body in this frozen ground either. Both women would be found in the river by the police force, its members more numerous than the fish. That seemed fine, preferable even. Goodbye to Gary. But she felt bad for her mom. She was finding peace floating away from the pollution, except for the lunacy of Rich's warped high-pitched voice, screaming like an idiot.

X

by Angel Luis Colón

Matt's kind enough to offer a drive to work this morning, which is weird, but welcome. Normally, he's the prototypical doting husband, but he's usually in a hurry and I'm the patron saint of perpetual tardiness. We aren't morning people, so at least it would be a quiet drive. Better yet, it's my first time in the new Beamer. Always loved the new car smell—glad it isn't gone yet.

"You mind some music?" He turns the radio on before he finishes the question.

"Whatever." I'm in a mad dash to finish grading the last few papers on my pile. The only reason I accepted the ride was to catch up. If I'd taken my own car, I would be doing these five minutes before the kids started piling into homeroom. Geraldine, one of my coworkers, can always drop me off on her way home. Whatever, that's for later. Papers now. The outside world and the fact that my panties are more than likely on backwards need to come in second and third respectively.

I do my best to keep from looking at Matt. That's been the case all morning. "Sorry I'm so anti-social. I need to concentrate on finishing up." Not even seven in the morning, and a bead of sweat forms on my neck and crawls down my back. I tied my hair up, but it doesn't help. I need to chop it all off as soon as I get a chance. "Air conditioning would be great." I mark another wrong answer with a red X. "These kids never read the material thoroughly." I'm talking more to myself than to him.

"Well, you're good with them, Michelle. It'll get through." Matt's words come out robotically—his volume lowers when he hits the end of the sentence. He pulls the car out of the driveway. He keeps clearing his throat.

"You okay?" I ask.

"Yeah, I'm fine."

I lift the graded sheet—a 60 out of 100—and place it on the center console. It folds over the faux black leather. Move my pen to start grading the next paper, but the sheet underneath isn't one of the tests. My throat and mouth go dry. Feels like I'm chewing on cotton swabs.

Matt looks over to me. "What's the problem?"

I lift the paper up. It's a zoomed-in picture of someone's cock—not just someone—I know whose cock this is. "Where did you find this?" I hold the picture between my fingertips at the top. Can't bear to look again.

He laughs, turns up the music—it's Stevie Wonder, the first song that played at our wedding reception—*Ribbon in The Sky*. "Where did I find it? You've got the nerve to ask me where I fucking found that." Matt stares ahead at the road.

Dropping the picture to the floor, I reach out to touch his shoulder, but I can't find it in myself. "I was going to tell you about this, just didn't…baby, this is very much not what you think it is." I realize he's wearing the same clothes as yesterday. There's a faint smell of bourbon I hadn't noticed before. "Are you drunk?" I lean over and sniff to confirm the smell is coming from him.

"Very." He swerves the car back and forth with a chuckle—the way he used to in college. "Don't worry, though, I won't make any bad decisions. Not like you."

My ears go hot the way they do when I'm mad or nervous. "Pull the car over and let me explain…" I reach over to the steering wheel and he shoves my hand away. "God damn it, pull over and let me drive. I'll explain."

Matt smiles tight. "Explain? What? About how one of your *kids* sent that to you?"

I rub my eyes. That only makes them burn worse. "It was a prank; I already forwarded it over to Lisa so we can look into the issue." I feel the first tear slide out and down my cheek. It finds a home under question three of Marcia Adams' test. She always gets hundreds.

Matt speeds up. Wipes sweat from his forehead. "Bullshit. I read that message a hundred times last night. It was from that little motherfucker you're always going on and on about. Neil, right?"

This again. "Because he's a problem student." The song ends and starts again—a melodic hammer to get the point through my skull. "Can we shut the music off?"

He places a hand over the radio console and side-eyes me. "Yeah, real problem student for you, huh? Is he even legal? Are you some kind of a pervert now? Is it that I'm too old for you?" He spits as he speaks. "What would possess you to do this kind of shit? It's insane. We're going to end up like those people in the news." Matt wipes a hand across his bald head. All that drinking kept him from a shave. I can see the shadow of his monk's hairline. "What were you thinking?"

"Holy shit, this is far and away not what you think it is." I look out at the road. We're going way too fast. Hope to God there's a speed trap or a nosy old neighbor out walking their dog—something to get this to stop. "Just stop the car and we can talk. I told you…"

The gun is against my cheek in the blink of an eye—cold, steady. I can smell the oil he uses to clean it. It's his favorite piece, the .45. The safety is off, but his finger's not hovering over the trigger. There's still hope.

"How could you?" Tears spill from his eyes. "Do you have any idea what you're doing to me?"

"I swear to God, it isn't like that."

Matt forces the gun harder against my cheek. My head thumps against the window. Pain shoots from the cheekbone up to my eye socket and into my ear. "Then what is it like? Tell me." He ignores the road. *"Tell me!"*

Neil Paulsen—class clown extraordinaire, troubled student—stood at my desk with a shit-eating grin on his face. "What is it now?" He had the same look most of the other boys his age did. Semi-long hair combed to the right, flannel shirt, skater shorts—the uniform of the desperately "individual." He was as fit as most of the jocks, but didn't play sports. Around the school, I'd heard him pegged as a stoner—a waste of space. Hearing that kind of bullshit pissed me off. All it took was effort and nobody would be a lost cause.

I leaned back in my chair and sighed. "Neil, this is the fourth time you've disrupted the class during a test—the fourth time I've given you detention."

"So?"

"So? What is it going to take to get through to you? You're a smart kid, I see it. You're not lost with the material, you're bored."

"Well, yeah."

"Why?"

He shrugged. Amazing how apathy never managed to go out of style.

"So you're going to let your grades suffer for it—drive everyone insane because you're bored?"

Another shrug.

I watched him. Understood why he was against anyone over 21. I was a kid too—they forget that—all of their teachers were once kids too. The baby fat was just fading on his cheeks. In a year, he might even need to shave the fuzz that patched his upper lip, cheeks, and neck.

"No answer?" I went back to my ever-static pile of papers. Waved him off. "Go home, then, I'm tired of this."

Neil turned and headed to the classroom door. He lingered a moment and turned around. "What if I did something for extra credit?"

If I didn't will it to stay closed, my mouth would have slacked open as if I had a stroke. "Are you serious?"

He nodded. "You're right. I know most of this stuff. What if I wrote a paper or something…on a topic I choose? Would that pick up my grade?"

"Seems fair enough. And yes, it would help your grade." I placed my pen down and folded my hands on my desk. "Pitch it. What would you write about if you had a choice? What historical event interests you enough to write me a well-researched paper?"

His eyebrow raised and he bit his lip. "I read a story about Lincoln's kid being saved by the brother of the dude who shot him, that seems interesting."

I nodded. "That does seem interesting. How about, say, fifteen hundred words by Friday? Email it to me." I wrote out my Gmail address—separate from the school's to avoid any BS about "unauthorized subjects" or special treatment. I had enough headaches defending half of my lesson plans because they didn't meet the "criteria."

Neil smiled and took the slip of paper. "Sure. By Friday. Thanks, Misses Gonzalez." He jogged out of class.

"Anytime, Neil. This is what I'm here for."

I stared at my papers for another ten minutes and got nothing finished. I felt great—inspired even. For the first time in my six years at Madison High School, I actually reached one of them. The papers could wait until later. Matt was working late, so I decided to treat myself to a fancy burger dinner—even a beer.

Walking out of the school, I noticed Neil standing with a few of the other misfits in the parking lot. He gave me a nod and went back to talking to his friends in his animated manner. Showed them something on his phone and jabbed his finger at the screen excitedly. Heard them all break out into fits of hysterics over one of his stories.

Good kid, all he needed was a little push.

Couldn't sleep, so I decided to check my emails. Matt wasn't home yet, sometimes it worked out that way. No news was good news. I booted the laptop up, snuck into the kitchen for some leftover fries and another beer, then sat down to read the messages. Pretending to get work done did wonders for putting me back to sleep.

There was an email from Neil marked as 'read,' which was strange, because it was sent around 7:30 PM and I'm damn sure I was watching Netflix in the bedroom around then. I chalked it up to a hiccup in a server somewhere out west and opened the message.

I should've stayed in bed. The email read:

Michelle,

Missed you so bad today. Couldn't stop thinking about us together. How about you have a 'conference' next week and get away from that loser husband? Then we can do something about this.

I scrolled down—another mistake. It was a picture of Neil, smiling and nude. His right hand was wrapped around a member that had to be Photoshopped.

Snapped my laptop shut as if it bit me and pushed my chair back. Fries and beer spilled at my feet, but I ignored it. Too busy trying to erase the image from my mind, but it was stubborn, burned into my retinas as if I'd stared at the sun too long. The question kept popping up—why? Why would he do this to me? Why would he think this was a good decision?

There wasn't time to sit and think it through. I opened my laptop again and forwarded the email to Lisa McAffrey, my principal. I changed the subject line to include a huge warning about the content, and wrote a near novel's worth of explanation. Hopefully she could do something. I mean, my only mistake here was trying to help. How could I have possibly known Neil would do this? I switched back to the original email and found myself staring at the photo again. At his muscular chest, his abs and the most impressive part of the package—for lack of a better word. I bit my lower lip and felt the skin around my neck getting hot and flushed.

No, this was wrong.

I deleted the original email and picked up the phone. It was too late to actually call Lisa, but maybe I could give Matt a call and talk it over with him. He might know what to do. I realized my hands were trembling when I called him. Wasn't sure why, I wasn't scared.

Matt didn't pick up. I waited for his voicemail and spoke at the tone like the lady in the recording told me. "Hey babe, um, it's almost eleven. Can you call when you get this message? Not sure if you're sleeping in the office again or if those planning meetings are getting as bad as the last launch did." I paused. I wanted to tell him about this mess so badly, but over voicemail? No, we had to talk about it in the morning before I headed out to work. "Anyway, love you. See you soon." I disconnected.

There was no way I could stay next to the laptop or even dream of looking at students' papers, so I went back to the bedroom. Went back to the marathon of *Orange is The New Black* and tried to not think of the picture, of Neil's member and his body. Fucking hell, was he even eighteen? Had to get my mind off of it. Tried to watch Piper chase a chicken for the second time, but it didn't help. If anything, the chicken made my mind wander to cock, which made my mind wander to something worse.

I jumped out of bed. Tore my clothes off, ran into the bathroom and hopped into the shower. Extra-hot water helped to melt the stress away and I leaned against the cool tile. There were butterflies in my stomach. I closed my eyes and lifted my head, let the water hit my front. Opened my eyes stared at the showerhead. Realized it was a handheld model. I reached up and detached it. I ignored the guilt, set the stream to 'pulse,' lifted my leg and rested my foot the soap dish. I thought about Neil and aimed the showerhead at the spot that needed the real attention.

"Tell me," Matt growls.

"I did. I gave him my email for an extra credit assignment and he sent that…that thing as a sick joke. I swear to God, Matt. I was sick when I saw it." My heart pounds so hard I swear I can see my blouse shifting. "For fuck's sake he's a kid and I'm a married woman. I'd never do something like that."

Matt's demeanor softens, but the gun doesn't lower. "You didn't even think of it?"

"Jesus, no," I lie.

He watches me a moment and his eyes harden up again. "You're lying." His foot weighs down on the gas until it's touching the floor. He sets the cruise control and shifts his weight to press the gun against my face hard enough to push it against the side window. "So maybe you didn't fuck him yet, but you liked what you saw didn't you? Maybe you guys would trade a few more snapshots then you could run off behind the bleachers or something. Was that the plan?"

"Matt…please." A car swerves by on my side—the driver leans on the horn. "Oh God, Matt, please. Just…pull over. Pull over before we get killed."

"Stop deflecting the question."

"Deflecting?" My breath fogs the window. "You're not watching the road."

"Did you think of it?" He bites his corner of his lip the way he does whenever he gets mad.

"We're gonna crash."

"Did you fucking think of it, Michelle? Answer the goddamn question."

"Please. You're gonna kill us." I look from Matt to the road. We're swerving between lanes and edging closer to the oncoming lanes.

He takes a long breath. "I swear to god, you don't answer the question and I'm gonna shoot you in the face." The barrel of the gun slides down my jawline and rests on the side of my chin. "Right here—so you can feel it." His finger slowly slides over the trigger. "Answer. Did you or did you not think about that little motherfucker's cock?"

I clench my eyes shut. "Yes," I whisper. "It was wrong. Just wrong. I don't even know why, for Christ's sake. Maybe it was the shock of it all. I…I'm sorry. I fucked up. I thought I got through to him—really through to him." I lean my head back on the headrest of my seat. The gun barrel follows. "There's nobody in this situation that fucked up more than I did, Matt."

There's clarity in Matt's eyes that wasn't there before and he swallows. "I don't…"

Another horn sounds off. Louder than before—bass to it.

A pop.

My vision goes white.

Matt lets out a loud hiccup.

I feel myself get pulled towards him and then back to the window. My head slaps against glass, and I feel a rush of air. It's cool against the warm wet on my face and arms. The papers on my lap tickle my neck, lips, and fingers. I can hear glass shatter—staccato music all around us. Stevie Wonder's hitting the crescendo of his song for the fifth time. None of the noise is in sync with him.

Then there's an earthquake and the grinding of metal against metal.

It's quiet. Can't feel my right side. I taste pennies. I blink and the road is out my window, cold against my hot face. It's raining…no…too warm for that. I turn my head the best I can. Instant pain—knives in my neck and the back of my head. I see Matt. His eyes still open, still clear, but staring right through me. Blood drips from his mouth and lands on my cheek. He's bent over the dashboard where the steering wheel should be. The white leather of his seat is stained from headrest to lumbar support in deep, dark red.

The pain fades away and I almost laugh when it all hits me, but I can't—my mouth won't listen to my brain. I want to move my arms, to shift in my seat, but my body's about as cooperative as my mouth. I listen to the cars as they pass by. Count them off until I hear them stop and there are footsteps. Someone calls out, but we can't answer—not anymore.

Neil's email is still on my lap. Stuck against my thigh—a wet, red, X keeping it there. Stevie Wonder starts singing through static and I close my eyes. I hope Lisa got my email. Hopefully, that will clear things up.

Shadows of the Mouse

by Garnett Elliott

Manero reclines in the highest tower of the Enchanted Castle, watching tourists mill under the sun-shot Anaheim haze.

The little turret's crammed with a bank of closed-circuit monitors and former LAPD officers, the latter sweeping the crowds below with Armalite AR-50's, alert for any suspicious activity in this—the Cheeriest Place on Earth.

"Eyes on. Got a lone male with a plastic bag, Future Land concession line."

"ID?"

"Running. Track him, meantime."

"Roger."

The AR's scope winks as it follows.

All this, Manero reflects, so some toddler can get dizzy in a giant teacup. He's sipping espresso from the tower's hard-pressed illy machine. Everyone here sips espresso. Maximum caffeination, minimum urination.

The phone next to his ergo chair rings. It's a landline, got a cord and everything, and the tone has been carefully muted so no one startles and takes a head off a thousand yards away. Manero picks up the phone and hustles it into a supply closet heady with the scent of gun oil. Closes the door.

"Hello?"

"It's you." There's a sigh on the other end that could be relief. A chair creaks. Manero imagines a corner office with a view only slightly less breathtaking than the Castle's.

"More trouble, huh?"

"She's pushing it. She's so pushing it."

"Another sex tape?"

"Worse. This is…run a search. See how fast it comes up."

Manero slips a more modern phone from his pocket. Pecks in the name 'Skyye Salinas' on a search engine and wades through the official sites. There. A blog called *Maraschino Paradise*. "I think I found it." The arbitrary content warning comes up, and then…

Pearlescent caverns. The pink stipple of shaved flesh.

"She's blogging about her vagina, for Christ's sake."

"Humble of her." Manero scrolls. "She used a pretty invasive camera, for some of these shots."

"It's got to stop."

"Slap a Cease and Desist on her. Sue for breach of contract, behavior unbecoming an Enchanted Kingdom employee. Something like that."

"Already talked to the legal snakes. She's eighteen, so she can post pictures of her hoo-hoo if she wants. As for contracts, she's in the middle of renegotiations right now."

"Which is why she's pushing it."

"Exactly. Holding us hostage for an extra two mil."

There's a buzz of excited voices outside the closet. Facial recognition software has made the Lone Bagman. No criminal record, but he has an Arabic surname. One of the ex-LAPD is lecturing about non-metallic explosive devices.

"Manero," the voice says, "I want you to handle the renegotiations. Personally."

He braces himself as he rides the tiny elevator down to ground level. Out through the security door, the tower's concealed entrance/exit, and he's wading through shoals of park-goers. It's impossible not to feel nihilistic in a SoCal crowd. Only a matter of time, he figures, before one of the snipers goes futz-o and starts mowing down the sheep they're supposed to protect.

On the way to employee parking, he spots what surely must be a sign. A tweener girl, bored or stoned, eating pale blue cotton candy. She's wearing a Skyye Salinas t-shirt. It's from several years back, when Skyye's sitcom *Way to Go* was pulling in eighty-five million viewers worldwide. Making bank for the Mouse.

That was before her auto-tuned faux-country album hit. And *Way to Go* vanished in spinoff land.

Child stars as radioactive waste. Now he understands why.

Hostile press already has Skyye's Brentwood estate surrounded, but she never spends much time there anyway. Five bills to a certain cleaning lady at the Four Seasons yields better results: a wadded-up printout depicting a Vegas hotel, found in the wastebasket of Skyye's usual suite.

One theme park to another.

There's a flight leaving John Wayne for Vegas in fifty. He stops at his home on the way to get some things. 'Home' is a studio apartment, a cardboard armoire and a worn futon from a time when people still slept on futons.

His significant other lies coiled in one damp corner. Simba, a Burmese python, knotty and lethargic from her last meal. She recently graduated to guinea pigs. He knows some velvet morning he'll wake in her embrace, waiting for him to exhale so she can tighten. A fitting end, really.

The snake was his therapist's idea.

About an hour from LA to Vegas, long enough to shudder up into the clouds and come angling down again. The metallic ding of slots paying off echoes as soon as he de-planes. His life's theme song: someone else getting lucky.

A taxi drops him at the strip. He turns, squinting into the Nevada blue. Across the street looms the hotel from the wastebasket. The Caravel.

It seems right at home next to the black glass pyramid. Some fantasy version of a seventeenth-century Spanish galleon, with too many decks and neon portholes. The sails double as giant projection screens. Flickering lasers advertise the floor show and Buccaneer's Buffet. But for all that, if the wind blew right, if the gilded anchor lifted, the whole thing looks like it might go scraping down Reno Avenue.

Stepping into the lobby, he's aware of cameras under smoked glass domes. The concierge staff are all dressed like pirates. He's got a lanyard around his neck with a plastic badge, identifying him as EVENT STAFF—events being ubiquitous in Vegas. Despite the camouflage, he panics as he approaches the casino floor. It's the crowd. It's always the crowd. He pushes past a senior toting an oxygen bottle and beelines for a restroom, unsure if it's the right gender.

There's a male attendant inside, hovering over a selection of combs, towels, and bottles of cologne, ready to proffer, to advise. Manero fixes him with a look. A by-product of chronic insomnia, he can give soul-chilling looks. The attendant's smile fades.

Manero closes a stall behind him. Flimsy barrier, but already his breathing has started to slow. He makes a tactical decision and takes two forty-milligram propranolol tablets from his pocket.

When the stall door opens again he's another person. The attendant blinks at the suaveness oozing out of him, an aggressive courtesy honed from years in the entertainment grind. He tries a spritz of travel-sized Goti, sniffs, and pockets the bottle. A pair of twenties slithers into the little man's hand.

"I don't want to come across like a tourist here, buddy, but my wife insists there's some famous people in the hotel. You wouldn't know anything about that, would you?"

The badge seems to work with the help, but it won't protect him from security. And he knows they're there, nuzzling like sharks around the casino floor. He evades them with a sort of feral intuition.

Looking lost, maybe a little buzzed, he wanders near the kitchens. A balding Filipino carries a tray heaped with tiger prawns. Sight of the curled orange shapes makes him stop—aside from junk food, Skyye only eats shrimp. He falls in step behind the guy. They enter a service elevator, Manero careful not to make eye contact. Up seven floors and the door dings open. Filipino breaks left, Manero goes right for thirty paces down a lushly carpeted hallway, doubles back and finds the tray on the floor next to suite 707. 'The Captain's Cabin,' according to a brass plaque screwed into the door.

He hesitates. Did the guy just knock and leave? What's his story going to be if this is the wrong suite?

Improvise, improvise.

Before his knuckles can touch the door, it opens a crack. A bloodshot blue eye peers out at an imposing height. Looks at the tray. Looks at him. Narrows.

"You're not with the hotel."

Manero grins. "I'm here to talk to Skyye. Settle her contract."

"Where's the money?"

"This isn't a drug deal, friend. If she agrees to the terms, signs, all I have to do is call the Mouse."

"You don't have to be a dick about it."

"Just ask her. Please."

The door shuts. A moment later there's muffled conversation. Sharp words. The door cracks again, and two eyeballs appear this time. The second one's also blue, also bloodshot. Not as tall, though.

"I know him," Skyye's voice says. "How'd you find us?"

"Were you really trying that hard? Let me in and we'll talk."

"Search him, Lee."

A pair of muscled arms beneath a terrycloth robe reach out, pulling Manero into the smell of stale cigarettes and KY. He's shoved towards a bathroom the size of a small apartment. Pink marble cool against his face as Lee folds him over a sink, his free hand searching in brisk, professional movements.

"Why would I be armed for a contract negotiation?"

"Not weapons," Lee says. "Recording devices." Finished, he turns Manero around. Lee's been Skyye's personal bodyguard for the past eight months, well beyond the usual shelf life of her fuck-toys. Manero read the précis on him. Dishonorably discharged from the Corps. He'd punched a French photographer in the gut during Skyye's last visit to Cannes, causing a near-fatal internal hemorrhage. The Mouse's lawyers are still working on that one.

"You should be careful wearing these," he says, giving the lanyard a tug. "Someone might strangle you."

"It's breakaway. See the little clip?"

"Make it fast. There's some camel-fucker from Dubai calling in a little bit."

"Wants her in his harem?"

Shrug. "Says he's a big fan of *Way to Go.* So yeah, probably a pervert."

Skyye's chain-smoking in the main room. Enormous bay windows behind, making her a narrow silhouette against the Vegas skyline. The suite's a fucking pigpen. No staff in here for days. Plates piled up, stained sheets, clothes and towels in drifts on the floor. White-powder rails long as the Nazca Lines ghost a glass table. Red Bull cans. Skyye's not much for bathing, either.

She's got earbuds in, bobbing her head to something. Laptop nearby, screen glowing with the lurid colors of Maraschino Paradise. Her unwashed hair's been dyed so many times it's turned a grayish-green.

"Babe." Lee touches her shoulder. "Business, remember?"

Her eyes focus. Somewhere between angry and incoherent. She slips one of the buds free. Harsh, syncopated noise spills out.

Manero shakes his head. "She's down about fifteen pounds. We can't put her on camera like this."

"You fucks made her bulimic in the first place."

She kicks Lee's shin. "Stop talking about me like I'm not here."

"Skyye," Manero says, "my boss sent me. He's ready to deal."

"Was it the blog? Because I'm not going to stop. It's part of who I am."

"About that—"

"Here's the deal: I keep the blog. I get the extra money your tight-assed Armenian wanted to hold out on. And…I do another album."

"Skyye—"

"Not country, this time. Hip-hop. Also, I want a line of clothing."

"You have a line of clothing."

"For fucking thirteen-year-olds, yes. Starter bras and sequined shorts. I want something street, something couture." She pronounces it *cooter*.

"Mr. Avakian authorized the money, but he didn't say anything about albums or clothes."

"You tell him. Tell him he deals or the blog's going anal, next."

"Whoa, there." Manero puts up his hands.

"I'm dead serious."

"Alright. I'll call him now, but I'll need some privacy." He takes the phone out of his pocket and heads for the bathroom without waiting for approval. Lee doesn't try to intercept. Once inside, he closes the door but doesn't lock it.

The propranolol has kicked in strong now, so his fingers don't tremble as he slides out a length of braided monofilament from the lanyard. Lee didn't know how right he was.

He puts his back to the wall alongside the door and waits.

And waits.

After a while, heavy footsteps approach. Authoritative knocks. "I don't hear any talking in there," Lee says.

Manero's silent. He thinks of Simba.

When he was nineteen, barely older than Skyye is now, he auditioned for the lead in a slasher film. They shot actual movies in LA back then. He'd passed the first casting, gelled his hair up into a pompadour, and waited outside the office of Aryeh Schenk, producer.

The office door opened. A fat man ambled out, introducing himself as Mr. Schenk's personal assistant.

"You look nervous, son. Are you nervous?"

Manero admitted he was.

"Well, don't be. Mr. Schenk loves Italian boys. Come in and make yourself comfortable."

So he did. As this was the 80's, the office had pale neon on the walls and framed Nagel prints.

"You understand how this works? You're gonna have to spread. That, or suck him off. Or both. Hope you wiped good, huh?" He rummaged in the desk, produced a small bottle of baby oil. "Slather some of that on. When he comes in, first thing he likes to see is the old red eye. It's a submission thing. You can talk about the actual part when he's finished."

The fat man left. Manero debated his personal morals for all of fifteen seconds before anointing himself. Leaning over the desk, he fixed his attention on the drone of freeway traffic outside.

He waited with jeans bunched around his ankles for forty-five minutes, and when the door finally opened there was a chorus of laughter.

The fat man, of course, turned out to be Schenk.

They gave the part to Johnny Depp.

His foot's planted in the small of Lee's muscular back, pushing, while his thumbs pull with all his strength on the garrote. Lucky for him, Lee's only instinct is to try and dig his fingers under the tightening monofilament.

Propranolol is a tactical risk. It calms by deadening the fight-or-flight reflex, and that means no adrenalin on tap. Like a method actor, he conjures the memory of Schenk for the rage he needs.

Straining. He can glimpse Lee's face in the bathroom mirror. It's turning the same mottled purple as his own hands. Silent, except for the occasional grunt from Manero.

Then…

Lee's bladder goes. Warm piss all over the pink tiles. Sphincter too, but it wasn't the mess he was expecting. Small miracles.

There's no faking the absolute limpness that spreads over Lee's torso, so he eases the body next to the toilet. Rubs his hands until his circulation comes back. He searches under the terrycloth and finds a knife strapped to one ankle. That's military training for you. It's an SOG with a six-inch blade—perfect.

Before touching the handle, he takes a pair of surgical gloves hidden in his loafers and snaps them on.

Skyye's still at her bay window perch, earbuds back in, looking semi-conscious as she taps at the laptop. He approaches with hands in his pockets.

"Where's Lee?"

"Taking a dump."

"What'd the Armenian say?"

"He's alright with a new clothing line, but I really had to push for the album. Do you have any Xanax? I'm kind of on edge right now."

"Nightstand, first drawer."

He turns so she can't see the gloves. There's a half-empty scrip bottle under a thong, and he shakes out a handful. "What're you going to call the album?"

"I got to think of fucking everything? I don't know yet. I'll ask my fan—"

One latex hand around her neck. She tries to bite him as the other forces the Xanax past her teeth. Works the throat muscles to make her swallow, just like force-feeding a goose. Screams *mmmph* around his fingers.

Out comes the SOG. A pass over the carotids.

She pitches forward, letting out the last of her untalented essence.

After that it's like assembling furniture. All emotion drained except paranoia. Lee's body proves the hard part. He ties the garrote into a noose, secures it to the shower fixture, and manages, after several tries, to prop him in the corner and get his nodding head through the loop. The ligature marks don't quite line up. Also, because of Lee's height, his feet still touch the tiles. Sort of like he leaned himself to death. Oh well.

He squeezes the SOG's bloodied handle into a limp hand and gets a good set of prints.

Back in the main room, he snaps on a new pair of gloves, hiding the stained ones in his shoe. Skyye has thoughtfully left the blog editor open on her laptop. He types out the final entry for Maraschino Paradise, careful to explain her suicide pact using a fifth-grader's grasp of diction. Posts.

The hot-penny smell of all that blood is giving him a headache. He strips off his spattered slacks and shirt, both reversible. When he puts them on again he's dressed in stylish black.

Appropriate.

The flight to LAX is packed. So much so, he should be swimming through another panic attack. But thanks to two tiny bottles of whiskey, he's keeping his nerves at bay. Word must be flooding the net about the troubled starlet's last post by now. He wonders if they'll find the bodies before he touches down.

Across the aisle sits a perfect family of four, a snapshot from the 50's, the kids wearing round-eared hats with their names stitched in gold thread across the back. Dad's bragging about some app he downloaded, how it's going to cut the wait-time for all the rides at the Enchanted Kingdom. Mom just looks expectant.

Manero keeps his voice below the engine's whine. "I hope you people appreciate all the trouble I go through."

AUTHOR BIOS

ANGEL LUIS COLÓN's fiction has appeared in multiple publications. He writes book reviews for *My Bookish Ways* and is an editor for *Shotgun Honey*. He's been nominated for the Derringer Award and has won a writing contest or two. His debut novella, *The Fury of Blacky Jaguar*, is out this July.

GARNETT ELLIOTT lives and works in Tucson, Arizona. He's had stories appear in *Alfred Hitchcock's Mystery Magazine, Needle: A Magazine of Noir, Blood and Tacos, Shotgun Honey*, and numerous other online magazines and print anthologies. You can follow him on Twitter @TonyAmtrak.

DAN J. FIORE is a freelance writer from Pittsburgh with work published by *Writer's Digest, DarkFuse, Hot Metal Bridge* and *Thuglit*, among others. His short fiction won grand prize in the 82nd annual Writer's Digest Writing Competition and his screenwriting was awarded the Pittsburgh Filmmakers Institute's First Works Grant in 2009. He's currently pursuing his MFA. You can find more info and stories at danjfiore.com.

MATTHEW J. HOCKEY recently left a nice, stable, boring job in Northern England to teach Elementary English in Seoul South Korea. Though his days now contain more screaming and snotty noses, he finds it a hell of a lot easier to concentrate on writing. He has previously been published by *Shotgun Honey* and has short stories upcoming with *All Due Respect* and Comma Press.

MIKE MADDEN lives in Washington, DC. His work has been published in *The Saturday Night Reader, Pulp Metal Magazine* and in the *Baltimore Sun.*

AMANDA MARBAIS' fiction has appeared in a variety of publications including *Hobart*, *Joyland*, *The Collagist*, and *McSweeney's Internet Tendency*. She lives in Chicago where she is the Managing Editor of *Requited Journal.*

MICHAEL POOL is a writer and martial artist born in Tyler, Texas and living in Gunnison, Colorado. His debut crime novella, *Debt Crusher*, is due out February 15, 2016 from All Due Respect Books. Michael's fiction, satire and journalism have appeared or are upcoming in *All Due Respect, Out of the Gutter, Thuglit, Urban Graffiti, That Other Paper,* and *Rocky Mountain Chronicle.* When not writing, Michael teaches Brazilian Jiu-Jitsu to adults, teens, and children. For more information on Michael and upcoming places to find his work, check out his blog.

JOSEPH RUBAS' work has been featured in a number of 'zines and hardcopy publications including: *[Nameless], The Horror Zine, The Storyteller, Eschatology Journal, Infective Ink, Strange, Weird, and Wonderful,* and *Horror Bound Online.* His short stories are also collected in *Pocketful of Fear* (2012) and *After Midnight* (2014).

TODD ROBINSON (Editor) is the creator and Chief Editor of *Thuglit*. His writing has appeared in *Blood & Tacos, Plots With Guns, Needle Magazine, Shotgun Honey, Strange, Weird, and Wonderful, Out of the Gutter, Pulp Pusher, Grift, Demolition Magazine, CrimeFactory, All Due Respect*, and several anthologies. He has been nominated three times for the Derringer Award, twice shortlisted for Best American Mystery Stories, selected for Writers Digest's Year's Best Writing 2003, lost the Anthony Award both in 2013 AND 2014, and won the inaugural Bullet Award in

June 2011. The first collection of his short stories, *Dirty Words* and his debut novel *The Hard Bounce* are now available.

ALLISON GLASGOW (Editor) is all about that bass, 'bout that bass…

…no treble

JULIE MCCARRON (Editor) is a celebrity ghostwriter with three New York Times bestsellers to her credit. Her books have appeared on every major entertainment and television talk show; they have been featured in *Publishers Weekly* and excerpted in numerous magazines including *People.* Prior to collaborating on celebrity bios, Julie was a book editor for many years. Julie started her career writing press releases and worked in the motion picture publicity department of Paramount Pictures and for Chasen & Company in Los Angeles. She also worked at General Publishing Group in Santa Monica and for the Dijkstra Literary Agency in Del Mar before turning to editing/writing full-time. She lives in Southern California.

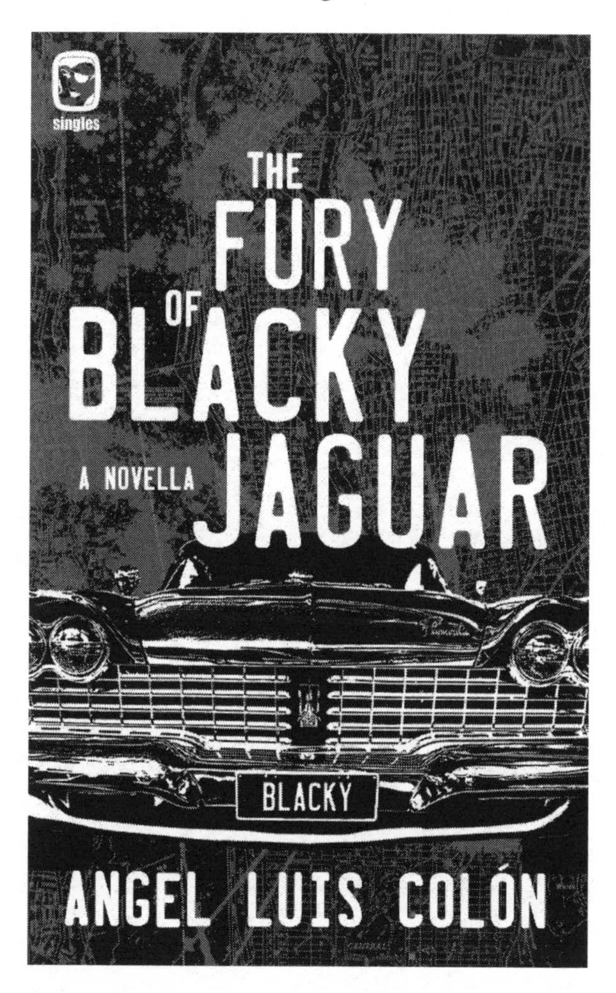

Blacky Jaguar—ex-IRA hard man, devoted greaser, and overall hooligan, is furious. Someone's made off with Polly, his 1959 Plymouth Fury, and there's not much that can stop him from getting her back. It doesn't take him to long to get a name—Osito, the Little Bear. This career bastard has Polly in his clutches, and Blacky doesn't have long until she's a memory.

Arthur lives a quiet life in London, wandering from the bar to the racetrack and back again. When his pension check dries up, Arthur decides to win it all back with one last big bet at the bookie. When that falls through, Arthur borrows money and repeats the process—until he's in too deep with a vicious gang of leg-breakers.

The repercussions are felt across the American South when a pizza joint in sleepy Lake Castor, Virginia is robbed and the manager, Odie Shanks, is kidnapped. The kidnapping is the talk of the town, but it's what people don't know that threatens to rip asunder societal norms.

Made in the USA
Lexington, KY
21 July 2015